THE CANYONS

THE CANYONS

BEN KOSTIVAL

Radial Books

Also by Ben Kostival:
Elm & North

Thanks to my wife, my family, Caterina Vidoli, Tadz Lewandowski, Marzena Lewandowski, Tricia Yost, Frank Soos, Rich Carr, Brad Paris, and Julia Masnik.

This book is a work of fiction. Any references to historical events, real locations, or real people are used fictitiously.

Published by Radial Books
radialbooks.com

The Canyons / Ben Kostival, 1st ed.

ISBN: 978-0-9984146-2-1

Typesetting services by BOOKOW.COM

For my family

"And at night, waking out of a dream, overwhelmed and bewitched by the crowding faces, a man perceives with alarm how slight is the support, how thin the boundary that divides him from the darkness."

ERICH MARIA REMARQUE, *All Quiet on the Western Front*

"And a man's foes shall be they of his own household."

MATTHEW 10:36

He brushed his remaining hand along the iron bars. He imagined the door blown down like a card, the bars forced askew from a blast. How much blackpowder would it take? Forget it, he thought. No fantasies of rescue. I am the last one left. All is as it should be. Behind me now. No need to review.

Nevertheless.

Months would pass before the town functioned again. And he had no doubt that the town would function again. Mr. Robertson would never abandon the investment. Everything would be rebuilt. To do otherwise would be to admit defeat. Not the old man's way. He would pay whatever was required.

Outside lay the mud. He could see it through the bars, through the wrecked wall. Tromped and cratered mud, a churning ocean of it. Occasionally a soldier walked across its surface. A savior, Baxter thought. A dirty savior. Soldiers. He had seen them before. Plenty of them. From the vantage of the cell, they came into view framed above by the lacerated and drooping eyelid of the roof.

None of it was worth another look. He knew what he had done. He knew what he and the rest of them had done, knew what they had created. There was no avoiding responsibility for it. He remembered with whom he'd talked of this. Another lifetime ago. They'd argued. He had not won, and Hawkins could not hear his concession now. With luck there was peace wherever he was.

Baxter did not hear any guards. Perhaps they had gone off somewhere to sleep, knowing he was in no condition to escape. After so much time in the tunnels—fighting, hiding—he could not keep from strategizing. The immediate problem remained unchanged: the cell was intact. The building was a shambles, but the cell was intact.

He was thankful it was dark again. With that, and if the guards left him alone, he might have an hour or so of sleep before dawn. He would need all the stillness he could gather. His stump had begun to throb again. Not much point in being well-rested for what was to come, but it always felt better to sleep. Perhaps he might be fed one more time before the end. There was a chance Dearborn would concede the gesture.

Absently, he scraped a bit of rust off the bars with his thumbnail. The bombs needed to be enlarged for metal targets. He had learned to be wary of metal. Too much bending. Metal is uncertain, prone to mixed results. Blackpowder just isn't dependable against it.

No more of this, he told himself. Sleep is the thing.

He sighed and shifted with pain. Months ago there had been a roof. Months ago a roof, along with everything else.

He tried to sleep.

1

Pick and shovel. He found them easily enough in one row, headlamp and leather helmet in another. The deserted stockroom was shadowed and silent as he kept scrounging, ignoring the reflex to hesitate. If he returned to the house even long enough to tell Lorraine not to worry, she'd either talk him out of it or he'd lose his nerve.

He moved deeper into the racks behind the counter. Coveralls. He unfurled a set and recoiled at the stench. He threw the coveralls onto his pile of gear. From the rows of reeking boots he selected a pair in his size.

He stripped down to his underwear and stepped reluctantly into the coveralls, wondering how their last owner had parted with them. Death or injury were likely prospects. He tried not to dwell on that. Instead, he fought to remember the standard equipment. Brass tags. A set of those went into one pocket. He checked the time. What he'd already gathered would have to suffice. He stashed his watch with his shirt and coat under the counter. He zipped up the front of the coveralls, collected his remaining gear, and left.

A short distance beyond the end of the alley lay a slag pile. Around its base spread a penumbra of debris. He gathered some dust in his hands and patted his clothing and face, clouding his skin. Then he bowed his head and kept his eyes to the dirt as he walked off.

Main Street held its usual traffic of miners and families, but he didn't think anyone took notice of him as he walked to the saloon.

Outside along one wall the men had stacked their equipment. He dropped his gear in the line. The wall quivered with the din from inside. Inhaling to steady himself, he walked around to the front entrance.

The space by the door was dense with men, and he could not properly step into the room. Rather, he leaned into the crowd until it yielded and absorbed him, and he made his way to the bar as if pushing against warm buoys. He coughed. The air was viscous with cigarette smoke. He placed a few coins on the bar, and when the bartender came to him, Baxter pointed at the gleaming, brass espresso machine. The less he was forced to speak, the better. In fact, he would prefer not to speak at all.

A loud slap came from somewhere within the crush of men by the door. The air jumped with shouts, and then the men began to exchange money. They dispersed and revealed a backgammon table already abandoned by the victor. His dark-haired, pomaded opponent remained seated, studying the formations on the board.

Baxter went to a small table in the corner, squeezing in against the wall. Only a few minutes left. Hurry, he thought, dismayed to see someone staring at him from near the door. Baxter's stomach pinched with tension. He dropped his eyes to his cup before risking another look. The man was still staring and, worse, was now moving toward him.

The man was thin and mostly bald. A swatch of hair, sallow as an old receipt, clung precariously to the top of his head. His large nose faded to the right and was flattened like someone had hit it broadside with a hammer. His ears folded sharply at their tops, and he kept his eyes on Baxter, pulling them away only to avoid colliding with other miners. Baxter steeled himself as the man reached the table.

"Are ya new?" the man said. He did not sit down. Looming over the table, he seemed unnaturally tall. His hands were scarred and thick with calluses. "*Jesteś tu nowy?*"

4

Baxter focused on his cup.

"Hey. *Neos? Novizio?*"

Baxter said nothing.

Another man came to the table. Baxter could see his boots on the floor. The second man said, "*Kto to jest?*"

"*Nie wiem. Jeszcze nie powiedział ani słowa,*" the first man said. "*Już próbowałem mówić do niego po polsku.*"

"*Hej!*" the second man bellowed. "*Mów!*"

Jolted, Baxter looked up, his hands trembling. The second man was heavier than the first, dark-haired and aggressive. He glared at Baxter, waiting.

"Maybe he's touched," the first man said.

"*Myślisz, że on jest szpiegiem Linda?*" the second man said.

Baxter's attention flitted between the two men.

"*Myślę, że nie,*" the first man said. "*Jest nowy na polu. Jego ręce nie wyglądają zniszczone. Poza tym czego Lind się dowie? Że nauczyłem go kopać w ziemi.*"

"*Uważaj na siebie.*"

"*Nie jestem głupi!*" the first man said. He pushed the other man away and faced Baxter again. "You deaf or something? A simpleton?" He snapped his fingers in Baxter's face. "Józef thinks your one of Lind's spies." The man wrinkled his nose and leaned in close, sniffing Baxter once and drawing back sharply. "You sure do stink. Christ. Like the undertaker is on your tail. That suit's gotta be washed out afore you put it on. Company ain't gonna do it for you. Man that wore it previous mighta had lice." Now he sat down. Without warning, he reached out and grabbed Baxter's wrists. The grip was like a door slamming on his bones. Baxter pulled back, but the man did not let go. He inspected Baxter's hands, twisting them around and yanking Baxter halfway across the table in the process, muttering, "Train another greenie. Like a blasted affliction."

The shift whistle screamed and the man said, "Shit." He released Baxter's hands as the saloon began to drain. Standing up, the man said with frustration, "Let's go, whoever you are. My name's Chamm. Eustas Chamm, if you can hear it. Stick by me and watch out you don't get killed."

Relieved to be on the move, Baxter fell into line behind Chamm as they went outside for their gear. Joining a column of men, they walked toward a contingent of guards who swung open the wire gates to a shaft. The men increased their pace, and toward the front of the line, someone tripped and fell. The line stopped as the guards pulled the man to his feet and kicked him on his way again. Passing the guards, Baxter hid his face under his tilted-down helmet. The main exhaust fan on the roof of the driftmouth whooshed deafeningly.

As the shaft sloped downward, helmet lights flickered on, pathetic in their weakness. Smaller tunnels branched from the main shaft, and the column fragmented. The side bores drew in tongues of five or six men. Baxter followed Chamm and four others into one of the shafts. The men bowed their heads for clearance. Then their shoulders stooped. Then their forward motion stopped altogether and the men set down their gear.

From what Baxter could see, the room spread out horizontally for twenty yards. The darkness allowed no certainty. The ceiling rose to only five-and-a-half feet on average, maybe six at its highest point. Baxter tried to turn about for a better look, but the movements of the team disoriented him. His skin moistened with sweat and his breath grew short even though he'd done nothing except nervously grasp and release the handle of his pick.

Near him, Chamm said, "We been working this stope off and on since the last round of blasting about a week ago." He rubbed his hand on the wall, flaking off a piece of rock. "The slate's as brittle as a whiskey bottle. Makes it easy to chop, but watch your eyes. The crumbs of it fly." He brought the shard of rock to his eyes and feigned pain for Baxter's instruction. "You picked a helluva day to show up. Today we're factotums. That's Lind's word. Said he found it in a manual. Know what it means? Mean's we're shit-all crew today. Yessir, today's a tour of the whole war. You want work, you got it." Chamm removed a pair of heavy rubber knee pads from his sack of gear. He held up the pads, prompting. "Ain't you got any?"

Baxter looked around as the sounds of the mine traveled through the tunnels—the grinding, indigestional thrum of a distant water pump, the screech of carts along tracks, the endless tamps of picks and scraping of boots, and every so often, a horrible, ominous groan from the pillars. The stirrings of panic heated his chest.

Chamm bumped him to recapture his attention. "Hey, boy, look at me. What about gloves? You got gloves?" He grabbed one of Baxter's hands again, slapped it a couple of times and waggled it before Baxter's face. "Gloves, dummy, gloves. I don't need 'em, but you got nothing but a little coon hand here."

Baxter wrenched his hand free.

"Suffer, then. You'll learn one way or another." Chamm snapped his fingers and pointed. "Hoist that pick, son." Chamm knelt, pulling Baxter down, too, and began to peck at the coal in a strip only inches above the rock floor. Baxter spaced himself off from Chamm and imitated his motions as all along the face the men chiseled into the seam and scraped at it with short-handled picks.

Instantly the room filled with dust. The headlamp became all but useless. The dust set his eyes aflame and he clamped his lids down in an effort to pump quenching tears to the sockets. Ordinarily he would have wiped his eyes clear with the back of his hand, but his skin was already covered with fine coal powder.

Baxter worked his way under the seam, raking out coal. The kneeling posture was uncomfortable enough when he'd begun, but it became ever more painful as, by slow degrees, the handle of his pick disappeared into the cutline. At the pick's farthest reach, Baxter's cheek was pressed firmly into the coal face. He found a grain of comfort in the fact that the work was numbing his mind if not his body, and by the time he was at the pick's depth-limit, his fatigue had pared away his fear. He extracted the pick and slumped on his knees for a rest.

"Hell no, boy," Chamm said without stopping his own work. "Word gets back to Lind that you're takin' slack time, he'll slingshot both of us out of the valley." He crawled away into the dust and returned with two sheets of metal molded like knights' breastplates. "Put one of these on. I'll show you how to use it."

Chamm scraped out the last of his cutline and dropped the metal sheet over his shoulders. "*Due trapani,*" he said, reaching out with one arm. From somewhere in the darkness a large hand-auger was passed to him and then a second one which he gave to Baxter. "Watch," Chamm said, and with the butt of the auger against the breastplate for leverage, he placed the bit on the coal face and turned the handle. He made only a start before measuring out a distance for Baxter, tapping the spot. "Right here. And when you're done with that one, keep cuttin' them down the face. One every two feet or so." His crisp, explanatory gestures were impressive and articulate. Alone, they would have sufficed for training, but Chamm did not seem capable of making them without speaking, too.

Baxter aped him once again, drilling a hole about two inches in diameter deep into the face. The logic of the task came to him. By cutting a space between the floor and the seam, they would create an overhanging ledge of coal. The holes they were now drilling would be filled with explosives, and when the charges were triggered, the suspended block of coal would fall into pieces to be collected. He completed five holes before he strayed too close to the man on his left, at least insofar as that man judged. He shoved Baxter away. Hard. Baxter flushed with anger. He turned toward the man, who had already dropped his auger, awaiting the challenge.

"*Smettila, Giovanni,*" Chamm said to the other man. "You were new and stupid once, too."

No use. He could not sleep, and there was no way to know how much time he had squandered trying. His stump throbbed heavily, which he hoped was not another hemorrhage preparing for release, and the ache in his arm spread through his body, collecting in the small of his back.

Through the wall came a breeze, nothing more than a wisp which licked him briefly and moved on. Bad, bad, bad. His clothes were wet with perspiration and humidity from the fleeting rain that had passed in the night. If the breeze intensified he would be cold, and there was nothing worse than being cold. He should stand up and be ready to pace. Not too long ago, the rain would have been snow. Either way. Of no importance. The desert will take its water any way it can.

He shuddered and wrapped the blanket around himself. He did not want to stand up. Sitting on the floor with his back to the east wall was about as comfortable a position as he'd yet found. Nonetheless, he forced himself to stand. His knees cracked as they straightened and took on the weight of his body. He swayed with the sudden change in orientation, bracing himself with his good arm. The concrete scratched coolly against his hand. He closed his eyes, breathing as evenly as possible. When he pushed away from the wall, the room had ceased spinning.

The breeze came again, carrying away the thin layer of heat which his body had built up beneath his clothes and blanket. He began to pace. He looked down at his feet. The boots had survived. The boots rode higher on the shin than the pair he'd borrowed for his first shift in the mine. The boots had kept his ankles safe. He remembered taking this second pair, remembered how he found them on the body in a remote tunnel. He'd thought only, This man is dead. He doesn't need boots anymore. That was all. A fact. No horror, just simple calculus. The man he'd taken them from? Nameless. One of the Italians who destroyed the water tower. The face was recognizable. The two Italians had departed, and an explosion had replaced the water tower. Neither man returned to the refuge rooms. One reached the mines again only to die of his wounds near the mouth of a far tunnel. Shot through the stomach. When Baxter stumbled across the body, he'd taken the boots. Then he'd dragged the body to the side so no one would trip over it.

Baxter watched the boots move back and forth across the floor. For a moment, his legs were a mere conveyance, somehow unconnected to his body. Quickly, he grew tired. He paused near the bars and suppressed a laugh. After all that's happened, he thought, now a few steps make me tired. There's life for you.

He looked through the bars, through the wall, to the mud outside. Still no sign of Dearborn. Perverse that he felt lonely for him considering what was to come. Dearborn had treated him decently. That still counted for something.

He tried to focus on his friends. He sent good thoughts after his friends. With the storm moved on now and the wind rising in its wake, conditions might be changing for them in the canyons. And beyond that in the mountains. And beyond that.

He thought of Garris. Somewhere with the others. They would be cold. The wind might be worse wherever they were, but they would have options: rocks, overhangs, caves. Make a fire. Wait. Move again.

They are still alive, he thought.

Hope. There was no harm in it.

2

At the end of the shift, Baxter climbed halfway to the surface before he realized he'd survived. Following the mules and carts up the main shaft, he dragged himself crookedly, favoring his side where a piece of slate had tumbled off a load and into his ribs. Daylight at the drift-mouth struck him like a swallow of brandy, material and calming, warmly seductive. New York's crowds, manuring horses, and automobiles had never so challenged his most basic functions. The shift had turned him into a blind man with an anvil on his chest. Now his eyes found the world again. He could not remember ever feeling such relief at the simplicities of sunlight and air.

He had not spoken in twelve hours. Foreign words spat at him by the other men did not qualify as conversation. The small amount Chamm had spoken made him an orator by comparison. Reticence was understandable. All energies had been dedicated to movement, effort. Words were for later when picks didn't need to be swung.

The men followed their loads to the tipple for weighing. A brass tag hung from each of the carts. Baxter rubbed his thumb across the matching duplicates in his pocket, which would be the sole way of identifying his loads. When he held his son's hand in Manhattan, he'd often felt horror at the thought of Thomas drowned by the tide of people, and now as he watched to ensure his own carts were not lost amongst the others, he felt a similar protective need. His eyes wandered from the carts for only seconds at a time.

Gradually, his thoughts returned to his actual duties. By his own estimate, he'd spent four hours, one-third of the shift, clearing waste rock from various locations. Four hours of chopping and moving slate. No pay for any of that, since pay was determined solely by the amount of coal produced. If a seam fractured in a difficult way, a man might go an entire shift with nothing to show for his labor. Dead shift. No question as to the effect on morale. Baxter would definitely recommend company policy be changed accordingly.

Long before they reached the tipple, Baxter could feel its presence in his feet. As the coal pounded and rattled through the sorters, the ground trembled as with the motion of a hundred streetcars. Previously, he'd only seen the tipple complex from the distance of the train depot upon his arrival. Now it awaited him, an assemblage of square buildings and towers suffused in a pulsing cloud of black dust, architecture all gray planes and right angles like unmarked dice thrown by a colossus. The line of carts and men wound forward through a range of enormous slag heaps that topped out with slack, rounded summits. Some of the piles smoked from within. Others leaked black tributaries of fluid.

Everyone followed the tracks into the weighing room. Baxter pressed forward with the crowd of men. On a platform beside the scales, the company security chief, Richard Lind, weighed each load and posted the result on a pegboard before issuing a man's appropriate scrip. Lind was only five years Baxter's senior, but the years appeared to have landed heavily on him. He was fleshier than Baxter, and his face was reddened in the way a sunburn takes to fair skin. When Lind frowned, his brows descended until they merged with his eyes to form a single dark line across the top of his nose. He spoke from a small mouth flanked by large jowls. Clothes of hard-worn canvas and wool covered his frame, and the overall impression of him was of blockishness. However, Baxter was not presumptuous. He knew he had not been in camp long enough to take other than

Lind's physical measure. He wasn't about to judge anyone's character based on two days of passing acquaintance.

One of the men scowled as his load's weight was posted. He glared alternately at the numbers and at Lind.

"If you don't like it, you can head out of the valley," Lind said. "There's always a train waiting."

The man took his scrip stub and walked off, disconsolate, and just then it occurred to Baxter that he hadn't thought through how to end his own ruse. If he stepped up with his cart, Lind was sure to recognize him.

Chamm's carts rolled next onto the scale.

"That's it?" Lind said. "You usually bring in five or six."

"Had to train a new man," Chamm said.

"Who?"

Baxter removed his leather helmet. To a mass turning of confused heads, he stepped onto the platform. "The scales?"

"They're not rigged. These men just think they work harder than they do. Don't jump to any conclusions."

"My conclusions are my own, Mr. Lind. If I don't inform you on every detail of my investigation, you'll just have to accept that."

Lind rested his clipboard on his hip. His finger flicked on the stack of paper. "What should I do with your load?"

"Issue my scrip to Mr. Chamm." Baxter said, groaning as he stretched his back, trying to do so without aggravating his ribs.

"Are you hurt?"

"It's nothing."

~

In 1906, when Baxter was only a middle manager, the company was victimized by an embezzler. The crime was first reported in the business section of the *Metropolitan*, and the exact amount of the missing funds was not specified. There was speculation that the amount was a pittance, not even worth old man Robertson's attention, but the opposite was also entertained—a shattering loss, tens of millions of dollars.

Wall Street tingled with gossip. Who stole from Paul David Robertson? The audacity! One might as well punch Andrew Mellon in the face and make off with his wallet. And more: in Mexico, Madero's coffers were suddenly flush from an anonymous donor. Was there a secret conduit for revolution inside PDR, Inc.? Pulitzer's muckraking *World* found delicious irony in the prospect. Robertson, after all, had contributed mightily to both T.R. and his rival, Parker, reasoning in print that with Debs on the ballot, it was wise to support both the Republican *and* the Democrat. Anyone but a Socialist.

Baxter followed the reportage, as susceptible as anyone else to sensationalism, and because he had no involvement in the crime and no connection to the alleged perpetrator—the company was vast, with one department having little to do with another—there seemed no harm in a bit of detached titillation. But the air of uncertainty persisted for weeks. Then the company's stock price fell on the exchange. Something had to be done to mollify the investors. In that atmosphere, Baxter received a memo from the old man's secretary. Mr. Robertson had requested a meeting. The memo was delivered on a Friday. The meeting was set for the following Monday.

Baxter's terror was immediate. He had always been scrupulous about keeping his division's books in order, but even the most careful man misses something from time to time. He wondered what error could be so dire as to require the old man's personal attention, let alone what disaster might ensue if his division proved connected to the crime. Over the weekend he walked around feeling sick, every now and then suppressing the urge to vomit. He could feel the axe blade on his neck, and at thirty he was not thrilled about trying to start over at another company. He and Lorraine had married only three years before. Thomas had just turned two.

Lorraine asked him, "Harlan, what's the matter? You look awful."

"I think I caught a stomach flu." At night, he squirmed in bed with insomnia and thoughts of imprisonment.

He collected himself as thoroughly as possible before the meeting. He wore a new collar, pristine and white, crisp against his cravat. His vest and topcoat were aligned and pressed. He smoothed out his trousers. His stomach was a single knot of tension.

Mr. Robertson's secretary, a thin man in his fifties, was dressed similarly to Baxter, but with finer tailoring. His topcoat draped more naturally across his straight shoulders, and he was at ease with himself in the famous receiving room. At an open file drawer, his hands moved quickly and with the fastidiousness brought about by long acquaintance with a task.

"Mr. Baxter, welcome. Please follow me."

Without ceremony he led Baxter into the huge, oak-paneled office. There before the billboard-sized window sat the great mahogany desk, the leather chair from which Mr. Robertson steered the company, and outside, the gray ravine of Wall Street, its buildings rising square against the sky.

The old man was not present.

"Mr. Robertson sends his regrets," the secretary said. He lifted a foot-high stack of folders from the desk. "He was called away on unexpected duties and will not be able to meet with you this morning. However, he is quite pleased with the work you're doing for the organization."

"That's unfortunate."

"That he's pleased with your work?"

"That he wasn't able to come. Please send him my regards. I was looking forward to meeting him."

"No, you weren't," the secretary said. "At least you wouldn't have been had you known the task reserved for you." He passed the stack of documents to Baxter. "The embezzlement which has recently become so public originated in our western holdings division. Our bookkeeping is therefore in need of quite a dramatic repair." He laid a hand on Baxter's shoulder, ushering him from the office.

"I'm not sure I understand."

"The head accountant for the western holdings, Mr. Baxter. He is a thief."

"How much has gone missing?"

"That's for you to parse out."

"Sir?"

"Over the last weeks we contracted for a company-wide performance review of all managers' past work. You proved to be the most efficient and error-free. It is for this reason that Mr. Robertson has selected you to rectify the situation."

"I'm being promoted?"

"For the time required for the task, yes. Mr. Robertson has reserved a decision on your long term prospects."

"Of course."

The secretary did not escort him into the hallway. "Those documents should be sufficient for you to start. You have complete authority to request other material as you think necessary. Comport yourself well."

"I heard someone disappeared to Mexico. I've read about sympathies with Madero. Is any of that true?"

The secretary looked at him, declining to answer. A wire of silence drew out between them until Baxter said, "It's of no importance. The company's primary concerns should be with the funds, with investor confidence."

"Indeed, and please know that Mr. Robertson does not delegate lightly."

"Thank him for his faith in me."

"Your record shows you to be thorough and resolute. Proceed in like fashion and I'm sure Mr. Robertson will be satisfied. Good day and good luck."

Baxter threw himself into the restructuring, conscious of its potential to improve his position. Nevertheless, the task proved a gigantic undertaking. Through five months he worked sixteen-hour days, demanding copies of ledgers from each subdivision and commandeering large, empty supply closets on the fifteenth floor to consolidate his work. Over three million dollars had been stolen. In the end, Baxter repaired the books across five western states by writing up a plan that covered losses with low-interest loans from friendly banks. In return, Mr. Robertson would have to guarantee small, five-year increases in accountancy services to the bank presidents' colleagues. Baxter submitted the plan, hoping that Mr. Robertson wouldn't find its naked reciprocity distasteful.

To Baxter's delight, the old man signed off without hesitation. However, Baxter was not promoted. He received a large bonus and a substantial raise, but his title and position remained unchanged. Never once in the process did he meet Mr. Robertson face-to-face. He received a letter—a formulaic note, in truth—which praised his loyalty and service and assured him that his diligence would not be forgotten. Monetarily, it certainly was not, but Baxter had been hoping to feel the old man's hand in his own, judge how much strength it had, look upon the countenance so brutally caricatured by the crusading journalists of the day—the aquiline nose, the gray hair pushed to the sides of the head like a crowd parted by a passing trolley, the tall and rigid frame often compared to his own buildings, and the green eyes said to be colored by the saturation of his blood with money. All rubbish, Baxter thought, but he wanted to speak from experience. He wanted to be able to unveil in conversation that, yes, as a matter of fact he'd had the opportunity to meet the man, and, no, of course he wasn't what the papers said. Who could possibly live up to his own caricature?

Baxter felt compensated by the reputation he gained as the old man's special assistant. Once or twice a year, Baxter found himself temporarily reassigned to work on a single project—rooting out a fraud here, researching a merger there—the duration and complexity of which was never predictable and whose successful issuance depended only on written reports submitted to the top floor. Each time, Baxter produced an unquestionable success, and each time, he received his concomitant bonus and raise. So, by the autumn of 1913, when a tunnel collapsed and killed three men in one of Mr. Robertson's mines, Baxter was not terribly surprised to be asked to travel to Colorado for a fact-finding mission. There was talk of a strike.

Niggers and poor men. Garris' words. Baxter understood them now. A shame, how long it had taken him. He took no pleasure in having come to see clearly. The lesson, though: Keep going. Just as Garris advised. Put your head down and go. For now, no more fighting, only movement. Yes, they had a chance.

Baxter was afraid to think so, afraid to invite bad luck. Still, Dearborn and the rest knew nothing of them. All dead to Dearborn. Baxter allowed himself a calculation. Twenty-five miles to the state border, after which, no militia. No more jurisdiction. How many killed before the flight? Seventy? A hundred?

One for sure.

Risks. Dearborn would return to Denver eventually, return to possibilities, meetings, debriefings, questions.

"Did you get his buddy?"

"Who?"

"His nigger pal. They were a team. You thought he did all that himself?"

What then? With so many bodies in the tunnels, on the plain, a straight answer would not reveal itself. Garris' body, unidentifiable even among the dead.

Far too late if ever, Dearborn would learn the truth. Far too late for a chase. The feds would not pursue a few stragglers. Garris was no

Geronimo. No quarter-of-the-army chase for Garris. Not if he kept his head down. Not if they all did. At least for a while.

Baxter kept imagining. Spring. The heat not yet deadly. The perfect time to run. No freezing at night, no roasting through the day. Enough melt in the brooks for water. South twenty-five miles to the New Mexico border, then another twenty-five southeast. The Sangre de Cristos, Taos, sturdy horses. For all he knew they were already through.

After that, timber camps in New Mexico. A rail ride to the silver mines in Nevada. Places enough, opportunities enough. South again, as good an option. Headwaters of the Rio Grande. Sante Fe. Albuquerque. Mexico, if they wanted. They could join Madero, join the revolution. Or not. Move away to some corner and start life anew. Who would recognize them? More migrants and wets. That's all they would be.

Niggers and poor men, just like Garris said.

3

Baxter doubted whether the house contained enough water for the wash-down he needed. The amount of grime that had built up on him from one shift was something hardly to be believed. He thought briefly about using the company bathhouse but decided against it. Too many questions would bombard him there. Even men who didn't speak English could hassle him greatly with gestures.

Lorraine met him on the porch. "Where in God's name did you disappear to last night?" She looked him up and down, aghast.

"I worked a shift in the mines."

"Why would you do that?"

"Research."

Worry electrified her. Her cheeks became red blades as they flushed across the underlying bone. Pulled back and bunned, her long black hair was a curtain drawn for the play of her face. She reached out for him.

"Don't. I'm filthy."

She grabbed his hands anyway. "Are you all right?"

"A little bruised. Mostly just exhausted." Theatrically, he raised his arms and rotated, displaying himself. "You didn't know you married a miner, did you?"

"I certainly did not." She stepped back and examined him again. "Harlan, you look atrocious."

Thomas came to the threshold and stood goggling by his mother. Lorraine said, "Why don't you ask your fool father what he was up to last night?"

Baxter squatted to meet the boy at eye-level.

"What happened?" Thomas said.

"I went to work. See what that gets you?"

"Dirty."

"I'm sorry I wasn't here to put you to bed."

Lorraine said, "We tried not to worry. Right, Thomas?"

"Mother paced a lot. I did, too, until I got tired. Then I fell asleep."

"Well, everything is fine now, but can you do me a favor? Can you check the level in the water keg for me?"

Thomas ran back into the house. His feet pounded on the floor. He reappeared in seconds. "Half full."

"Good. You can fill a few pitchers and bring them outside." He felt lighter as he waited on the porch for Lorraine to deliver him soap and a change of clothes.

~

The house was large and comfortable, but it lacked indoor plumbing. Attached to its side was a shower that was no more than a washtub on a high stand. The wooden stall enclosure barely cleared his shoulders and fell only to knee level. Other similar homes clustered about his, all of them empty, all of them knotted together on the plain beyond the town's southern limit. When Lind first admitted them, he'd said, "These houses are nicer than what we've got in town, but they never get used. The company built them thinking we'd have more city-type growth. Things in the valley have always been a bit unstable."

Baxter and his family made do, as they supposed everyone in the valley had to. It was the responsibility of the occupant of each dwelling to fill the large keg provided for water storage. Water was bought with scrip like any other commodity, but Baxter was at least exempt from this requirement. He could simply request a delivery, which he would have to do in the next day or so, given the amount of water Thomas ferried to him to fill the shower reservoir.

He closed the door and hung his clean clothes and towel over the top of the stall. He stripped and threw the dirty coveralls to the ground a few feet away. He felt a reflex of embarrassment. True, the stall hid what was important and no one else was around to see him, but how strange it was to be naked outside and in such a residential setting.

Above his elbows, the rolled-up sleeves of his coveralls had kept his skin relatively clean. In contrast, his hands and forearms looked as though they'd been dipped in black paint. He opened the valve on the screened outlet pipe. Shivering, he washed.

When he first told Lorraine that he'd accepted the Colorado assignment, the curve of her back tensed with anger.

"There's more," he said. "You and Thomas have to come, too."

"To Colorado? You're out of your mind."

"Lorraine, please."

"What will it be like there?"

"I don't know."

"How long would we be gone?"

"I don't know."

"Will we have a house? How about a school for Thomas? Will we be camped out under the stars?"

"I said I don't know!" He felt guilty for his temper. The questions were reasonable. He should have been able to answer them.

"I don't suppose you asked whether Thomas and I could stay in New York."

"No. It's against policy."

"This isn't one of his usual errands, Harlan. It's bad enough when he buries you in that office for months on end."

"He doesn't force me into anything."

"As if you could refuse? You'll just have to ask for an exception in this case, or leave us here and not tell him."

"I can't do that. It would be untoward. Word might get back to him."

"Pardon, I forgot: 'Ours is a family company.' Let him send his own family. As if he'd ever found time away from his moneymaking to have one."

"Don't be unkind. We've benefited greatly from his hard work."

"It's decided, then?"

"I'm afraid so."

"When are we leaving?"

"As soon as possible."

In disbelief, she hurried up the stairs to pack, cursing Mr. Robertson in undertones. In the end it took them a week to make all the arrangements, but there'd been no complaint from the old man about the delay. The matter was settled now in any case. They were here. Baxter was engaged with his duties.

He worked the soap vigorously, scrubbing and sudsing his hair. He examined the wound on his side—no broken skin, just redness and swelling. Grime whorled momentarily on the tops of his feet before disappearing through the slatted floor and into the dirt. Despite the chill of the water, he relaxed, and when he was finished, he shook off and dried his head with the towel. Still goose-pimpled, he dressed and went inside. In the parlor, he sat down next to Lorraine on the couch.

"Was there enough water?" she said.

"Plenty."

"You could have strolled around naked so the air could dry you. That way I'd have one less towel to launder." With dismay, she noticed his hands. The cuts, prominent now that the coal dust had been removed, spread across his palms like red stitching.

She grabbed one of his hands for a closer look and Baxter winced with pain. "Careful!" he said, with more anger than he intended. "It's from pushing rocks around. Sharp edges."

"Why didn't you wear gloves?"

"I forgot to take them."

She hurried upstairs and came back with a bottle of rubbing alcohol, a towel, and a roll of gauze.

"Is all that really necessary?" Baxter said.

"These could already be infected. Turn up your hands."

He did as he was told. Lorraine stooped before the couch and moistened the towel with the alcohol. She pressed firmly on his palms, and Baxter clenched his teeth, sucking his breath in as the alcohol seared into the wounds. "What is that? Acid?"

"Remember it the next time you want to do something stupid."

She wrapped his hands with the gauze, leaving just enough of his fingers uncovered to preserve some dexterity. When she finished, she stood up and inspected her work.

Baxter flexed the tight gauze. "I feel like I'm going into the ring against Jack Johnson."

"Maybe he would knock some sense into you."

"Where's Thomas?"

"Upstairs. I put him to work on his mathematics."

Baxter looked at his hands, throbbing invisibly under the gauze. "If his future were in those mines, I'd be in despair."

"That bad?"

"It's so much worse than you can imagine. I had no idea."

"What did you think about down there?"

"Getting out." His eyes began to close, and Lorraine pushed him off the couch toward bed.

"I won't do it again, love," he said. "I promise."

"See that you don't. Get some sleep. I'll make sure no one disturbs you."

"I'm so tired, you could drive a freight train through the front door and I wouldn't hear it."

He yawned as he started up the stairs. He took off his shoes and climbed into bed, sighing with relief. In town, a shift whistle screamed as he fell asleep.

He puzzled over his death, but not over who would be the one to effect it. Dearborn, certainly. Not a task to be delegated. Good. Baxter did not want it delegated. Startling that I'd rather know my executioner than not, he thought. Another conviction he could not situate properly.

He did not worry over hanging. That method wouldn't be chosen. Risked a spectacle. Too visible. The old man would want everything finished quietly, as cleanly as possible. Minimize witnesses. A hanging, especially if botched, wouldn't fit the requirements. He imagined himself at the end of the rope, neck not broken, choking, tongue out and waggling like a spastic worm. Unacceptable. Therefore: shot. That would be the way. In appearance, no different from all the other deaths. His body could be dumped with the rest and left to rot. Clean and un-ceremonious.

He speculated about the ultimate moment. How quickly do bullets fly? Do they outpace thoughts? If not, he might see something just before the end as the lead tumbled through his skull, triggering visions, memories. For an instant, he might be five years old again. He might only glimpse yesterday. He might never feel a thing. Never even hear the sound of the gun. One moment light and life. The next, the black of a dropped sackcloth.

He was empty of religion. Not that he'd ever felt much of it, but enough to argue, enough to confront Hawkins about, enough to think something might await beyond death. Now? No. He had no patience for any words on an afterlife. If he had even the slightest hope of seeing Lorraine and Thomas again, he would not have done as he had.

Let us recognize things for what they are, he thought. Let us name their parts. Nearly my whole life passed before I was willing to do so. These last months. A time of unveilings, a difficult education.

He considered Hawkins then, recalled something very like admiration, yet short of it. Not respect. He could not conjure a proper word. The quality was of a demand for thought, of insistence. Yes. One could not turn away from him without reckoning. He was unavoidable. For a time. And he made himself so with just a voice and a refusal to move. But of course in the end he had been moved. Lind saw to it, clearing him away as one might a leaf from a sidewalk. Too much, he thought. We can't take it all in.

If I had time left, I would remember him properly. At our beginning, his vision, a thousand times darker than mine. I came to his with time, which somehow he enjoyed. How? The same vision causes one man to kill, another to weep, a third to do nothing more than stand his ground. Chamm saw and smashed forward, headlong. Garris, too, more calmly, though, more methodically. The cool-headedness that age can bring. The valley shuddered and burned and Garris moved along when his chosen battle expended itself. And me. Given time and supplies, I was willing to do the same and more. Now all of it leads up to a single shot.

The frigidity of the analysis depressed him. To be capable of such logic was not heartening. Bad enough that my actions were a killer's actions. Now my thoughts are a killer's thoughts. I used to think like a man, act like a man, not like a killer. Too little time left to contemplate the difference.

4

He slept until four the following morning, waking with a pain below his left shoulder blade and an ache through his lower back. He rose from bed and gathered the clothes he planned to wear that day. He crept out of the room without waking Lorraine and went downstairs. In the kitchen, he draped his clothes over the wooden chair at the table. Fighting his gauzed hands, he filled a small pot with water from the keg and lit the kindling under the burner to make coffee and oats. He didn't need to rush. Dawn would not arrive for a couple of hours, and except for the soreness, he felt rested. He was happy for time and silence to eat his breakfast and dress for work, fumbling a little with his buttons. He planned to spend the day fashioning a preliminary outline for his report. His thoughts began spontaneously to organize themselves until they were interrupted by someone at the front door.

To Baxter's surprise, Lind stood on the porch. A rifle was slung across his back, and he carried a shotgun casually in his right hand. "I was headed out hunting. Saw some movement in here and took a chance you were up. Care to join me?"

Baxter's midsection was in line with the barrel of the shotgun. He stepped onto the porch, but Lind turned with him and the weapon's alignment did not change.

"Food's pretty routine in town," Lind said. "I like to bust up a few jackrabbits when I can. Rockchuck is good, too." His many-pocketed vest swelled here with shells, sagged there with empty game compartments. Two canteens were clipped to his side.

"It's still dark," Baxter said, disoriented by Lind's presence. Again, Baxter moved out of the way of the shotgun, and this time the weapon did not follow.

"Dark's the best time to walk in the desert. The more light, the worse for us. Soon after dawn, there won't be much point."

Baxter held up his wrapped hands. "I'm afraid I won't be much good with a gun. And I should be getting ready for work."

"We can spare the time. Even if we're a little late, the shifts should start up fine."

Acquiescing, Baxter looked at his shoes, which he'd chosen for a day in the office. "Let me put my boots on first."

~

They set out beyond town. Railroad track lay across the land in loose webs. The outline of a water tower, distinguishable against a backdrop of stars, rose from the top of a small hill to the south. Slag piles bared their shoulders on the northwest horizon. Baxter licked his lips against the dry air, squinting back toward the bluffs hidden by the darkness. During the day, the mine entrances resolved themselves on the culm-laden slopes, and the barbed wire which fenced in large portions of the property showed itself like spider veins on a pale thigh. High on the same inclines, miners burdened with picks and shovels would with the coming of light emerge from their clusters of housing. But now, wrapped in dark and distance, the mine properties felt abandoned, the valley at rest. And pressing on, the long-defunct length of track guiding the way became the only evidence of settlement. Then, even the track disappeared as Lind and

Baxter veered from it, climbing a rise while the track sunk into the lie of the plain.

Lind apparently felt no desire to talk while leading. Toting the rifle, Baxter contented himself with the sky and its innumerable stars. He could not accommodate himself to the aridity of the area. His lips had roughened, even cracking and bleeding on some days, and the desert scrub, which upon his arrival he'd not found remarkable, now struck him as astonishing for its ability to survive at all. Periodically he drank from the second canteen, but he could not quench his thirst. Wisps of dust rose from the fabric of his pants, and he was dismayed at how quickly eroded was the care he'd taken in dressing.

They walked until the darkness fell into retreat. As dawn pressed on the eastern sky, two jackrabbits broke from a clump of brush not far ahead of them. With a smooth and natural motion, Lind swept the shotgun to his shoulder, released a hoarse explosion, then adjusted and fired again. In succession, the rabbits tumbled over themselves and skidded to a stop.

"Well done," Baxter said.

Lind opened the gun, folding it in half and handing it to Baxter. "Pull those shells out."

Because of his bandaged hands, Baxter fumbled with the task, singeing his fingertips on the shell casings.

"Careful," Lind said. "They might still be hot."

Baxter licked his fingertips and tried again, this time with success, dropping the casings to the ground. He handed the gun back to Lind, who reloaded as they came upon the first rabbit. A few small, red holes tainted the white underbelly of its fur. The second rabbit dripped with blood and was still moving beside a fist of sage.

"It's not dead," Baxter said, looking on with difficulty.

Lind bent to one knee, grabbed the rabbit by the hind legs and slapped it hard against the ground. "Is now."

Uneasy, Baxter turned his attention in the direction of town. Only the vague profiles of the bluffs asserted themselves. The ridges formed brown and jagged sketch lines. He looked back at Lind, who had pocketed the rabbits. Small dark stains grew on the fabric of the vest where blood seeped through and clotted. Lind remained frozen on one knee, his gaze locked on the far distance. Then, smoothly, as if slowly deflating, he sunk to the earth.

"What are you doing?" Baxter said.

"Come down here, calm as you can," Lind whispered, now fully prone. "Just like me. Don't stop until you can taste the dirt." He took out a small pair of field glasses and put them to his face.

"What is it?"

"I'll tell you when you're down."

Baxter did as he was told. Actually, he was happy to lie down. He was tired from walking and his clothes were already dirty. "Here I am."

Lind barely moved his finger to point. "Creep your head up just enough to see over the scrub. Scan south along the horizon."

Baxter tried hard to shield off the increasing dazzle of the still-rising sun. "I see nothing."

"You're going too fast. Pick up every inch of that horizon and turn it over before you put it down again." Lind passed him the binoculars.

Baxter slowed his scan, and this time on a long angle to the south, he saw something he'd mistaken for an abnormally large cluster of sage. Protruding from the shape was a long, thick neck, unmistakably creature-like. "What is that? A deer?"

"Antelope. There was a band of them around here a few weeks ago, but I hadn't seen any lately. We're lucky to run into this one. A couple more hours and he'll be in the bluffs somewhere or farther out on the top of a plateau. At night they come down into the basin, looking for water, but during the day they bed up as high as they can get. They like to look down on everything."

"It's not moving."

"Of course not. It's watching us."

In the clear, dry air, the white rump of the animal expanded. "Strange," Baxter said. "Its backside just flared somehow."

"Gimmee those binocs," Lind said. Baxter passed them back. "When they stand up their ass hairs like that, they're set to bolt." Lind peered through the binoculars again and then inched toward Baxter, grinding along in the dirt. "We got to hurry, but we still got to take our time. Understand?" With care and an economy of sound, Lind unclipped the strap from the rifle and moved only a foot or so to the side before raising up to his elbows and sighting down the rifle.

"Can you get a good shot from this far away?" Baxter asked.

Lind pushed out two long breaths. "A good shot doesn't matter. I can get *a* shot. You don't wait for better than that."

He fired, and the animal humped up, appearing to fold in two, gnashing at itself. Then with incredible speed, the antelope disappeared beyond the horizon.

"Did you kill it?"

"Calm yourself." Lind rose to his knees and took a pack of cigarettes from his vest. He lit up and drew in deeply. "If I hit him, we'll know soon enough when we go look for blood. If I missed, we'll have to wait him out. They're a curious sort. They'll stand and gape at you until they're satisfied, and if they're not, they'll circle back. If where he was standing was a good mineral lick, he'll be back for sure. On the other hand, if they take a mind to leave, they go so fast it's like you imagined them. Lie down and rest a while if you want."

Baxter drew up his knees and wrapped his arms around them. He looked at the sky and then at the ground between his bent legs. After a time, he said, "I feel all right, considering. I guess the walking loosened up my back."

"Hell of a stunt you pulled yesterday."

"Just doing my job."

"You're lucky one of them didn't put a pickaxe to you." Lind tapped the ground with the butt of the rifle, stamping out smooth oval shapes in the dust. "Don't be taken in by those rats, Mr. Baxter. You have no idea what they're like. Crooked as a bunch of Jews. And careless, so careless."

"They seem hard workers."

Lind closed his eyes and massaged them with one large hand. "You hear any union flap while you were dogholeing?"

"We were working too hard to talk."

"That's not it. They were suspicious. They didn't know you, so they kept their mouths shut."

"Regardless, I wouldn't have understood anything they said. Mr. Chamm was the only one I heard speaking English."

"Yeah, he's a character. A damned nuisance, too. One of him in the company is more than enough."

"If he's so much trouble, why don't you fire him?"

"Because he's useful. With all the foreign jabber, somebody's got to talk to the men. I can't do it. How about you?"

"No, I don't suppose I could."

"A lot of things have to be tolerated here that wouldn't be under normal circumstances. Chamm's one of them." Lind scratched at the dirt. "It shocked you, didn't it, what you saw down there?"

"Yes, but I learned a lot. I don't regret what I did."

"Those men have been digging since they were babies. It don't matter what country they come from either. Soon as they can stand, they stoop over with a shovel. Without a hole to hack away at, they'd be plain drunks. Just make sure one glimpse doesn't close the book for you."

"If I'd asked, would you have taken me in?"

"Down into those stopes? No way."

"Why not?"

"You're here to follow-up on an accident that killed three workers."

"That's right."

"And you're an assistant to one of the richest men in America."

"To put it crassly, yes."

"I don't care about crass. I care about true. And what's true is, you shouldn't expect men like me to take you places where you can get killed. Send you back to New York in a box? I've been in this valley a long time, but I ain't that crazy yet."

"I'm empowered to investigate fully. I need to deliver a complete report."

"I'll show you what you need to see, take you everywhere that's safe. Don't worry. You'll have more than enough information. I ain't looking to disappoint Mr. Robertson either. But you've got to understand, mining ain't a picnic. It's dangerous business. You got a whole mountain over your head. Sometimes it gets tired of standing up and decides to sit down."

"How did you get the bodies out?"

"Hauled them up in a cart. Best way to get anything out of those tunnels." He finished his cigarette. "See anything on that plain?"

Baxter grimaced, imagining a cart full of mangled corpses as he scanned for the antelope. "Nothing."

Lind got to his feet, dusting himself off. "Better start tracking."

They found a large blot of blood where they'd first seen the antelope. Lind pinched a bit of dirt in his hand and tasted it. "Salt," he said. "Should be a good spot until the spring rains."

Other drops of blood stood out dark on the tan ground. The trail was not difficult to discern, nor was it particularly long. They followed it for about a thousand yards before sighting the body. Even from some distance they could see that the antelope remained alive.

"Gut shot," Lind said. "Unlucky." The animal lay twitching grotesquely atop many square feet of ground blackened with blood. "Looks like I caught part of the hip, too."

As they came abreast of it, they could hear it lowing through wretched gurgles. Baxter gagged slightly, covering his nose and mouth. "What is that stench?"

"Fluid from the glands. I ripped through the intestine."

The mix of musk and feces was near overpowering. Baxter did not know how Lind could stand it, yet Lind only watched unperturbed.

"Aren't you going to finish him off?" Baxter asked.

"We'll let him bleed out."

"Show me how to use the rifle. I'll do it."

"With all that slop spread around inside him, the meat is ruined. Only thing left to take is the horns. They'll make a nice trophy. Maybe you can send them back for Mr. Robertson. But if you fire away, you could crack 'em. No telling where a bullet goes once it hits something. Besides, I have to order special for game this size. The ammo's expensive. No use wasting it on something that'll be dead soon enough."

The red mass of the abdomen convulsed. The antelope appeared to choke on its own fluid. "The company will resupply ten times what you need," Baxter said. "Mr. Robertson won't miss the horns if they're ruined. Please."

Lind considered him briefly, then pulled a large knife from his vest. The edge flashed in the sun. "Stick him in the throat if you want to get it over so bad. He don't look keen to run."

Baxter made no move for the knife. He only stood watching the animal's terrible endurance, wishing for it to expire.

Lind said, "I guess we wait."

The next minutes stretched to infinities that Baxter felt compelled to witness. Even in its shattered state, the antelope possessed great beauty. Its blood spilled downward from its stomach, and through stains of red and bile, the remains of its original colors held the eye. Semi-striped and spotted, the once-white belly graded to hay and buff halfway up the body-line and deepened to dark brown upon the back. The throat banded with brown and ivory to a white underjaw, and each ear topped an ink-dark spot. The white rear resembled, absurdly, a piece of exploded popcorn.

At last, the antelope fell limp and slack. Lind kicked it once to test for movement. He propped the guns on some sage to keep their muzzles from the dirt. Then he knelt down and rolled his sleeves up to his elbows. He drew his knife. "Take hold of the jaw and head."

Baxter pinned the head to the ground and held it fast. The fur was soft, the flesh sickeningly warm, the mouth still moist with spittle.

Lind worked with the knife, splitting the hide first along the underside of the neck. "Normally we wouldn't do this if we wanted to keep both the cape and the antlers, but those don't matter for us." He made another cut from a point on the shoulders, up the back of the neck to within inches of the horns. Beginning again at the shoulders, he sliced down toward the chest as far back as the centerline of the shoulders. Soft sheets of wet heat from the newly exposed meat lapped Baxter's face.

Lind's arms worked, painted with gore. "Bottom line is, they have to know who's boss."

Gagging, Baxter said, "What? Who?"

"The men. Can't let them forget for one second who's in charge." They rolled the carcass over, and Lind began a duplicate set of cuts that joined the previous ones under the chest.

To hold his composure, Baxter focused on Lind's boots. "We could think about a concession or two."

"Like what?"

"Mandate a few breaks throughout the day. Also, I spent a lot of time digging waste rock on my shift. Maybe a flat wage for that labor could be added to the scrip."

"Pay them for dead work? I'd be against that. We'd just be giving them an excuse to dig less coal. If they don't like what we pay, they can head on out of the valley." Lind's breathing thickened with effort. "Hold that head down."

Baxter leaned on the skull. "They've got no other demands?"

"Same as always: more pay, less work. That's what it comes down to. They want a union, but they ain't getting one. For some reason, they think a union is going to change the basic facts."

"And the threat of a strike?"

"It looked bad at first, but less now. Back to the usual grumblings."

Baxter peeked as Lind skinned away the hide beneath the junction of the head and neck.

"Believe me, I know what I'm talking about," Lind said. "I've seen what happens when you let your guard down. I was at Homestead."

A ripple of interest passed through Baxter's anxiety. "How close?"

"Right on one of the barges. I was in the first group they sent down-river to clear out the strikers. I'd just signed up with the Pinkertons. I was just a baby. Only twenty-one years old."

"I remember reading about it in the papers, hearing about it at school. That must have been something."

"If you ever want a good scare, get a couple of your friends to-gether and square off against ten thousand strikers. When the fighting started, I thought it was the Civil War all over again."

"Was anyone you knew . . ." Baxter stopped himself. "I'm sorry. It's not really my business."

"Killed?" Lind said. "Sure. Lots of others, too. And all the union folks got off because of friendly juries." He rose to a squat to reposition himself. "Almost done. You can let go now."

Baxter pulled his hands away as from a hot kettle.

"I don't like it any more than you do, Mr. Baxter, but I'm paid to be tough, and I plan to be, as much as necessary. If you give them a crumb, they'll take the loaf, and the next thing you know, we'll wind up with the goddam Socialists running the country."

Baxter stood and took a few steps backward. "Let's worry about the company before we worry about the nation."

"Yes, sir." Lind made a final crunching cut through cartilage and tendon and twisted the head free. "I gotta take the whole thing back. Can't cut the horns with this knife. I need a saw."

To Baxter's relief, Lind started toward town. Baxter toted both weapons while Lind carried the dripping head. A cloud of flies broke from the carcass to accompany the trek.

Morning had not fully passed, but already the sun was hot. Baxter could feel himself wilting. His boots were not properly broken-in, and his feet had begun to throb. They were taking a different tack home, and along the way he spied the ruins of a small shack in the distance. One wall leaned precariously as if the sun had pummeled it from the vertical, a loose plank hanging down like an arm stretched out to arrest its fall. Perhaps the shack had once been a switching station or a supply shed. Had he not been so eager to reach home, he would have suggested a rest in its shade. But they pressed on. Baxter took a handkerchief from his vest and mopped his face with it.

Lind drank deeply from his canteen, and Baxter, his head listing with heat and light, asked, "May I have a little of your water? I'm sorry. I feel a bit faint."

"What you had already will hold you. I need mine."

In time, the ugly line of town came into view again. The sun threw its light horizontally onto the wrinkled faces of the bluffs. Baxter had not seen them so emptied of shadow before, exposed now as if being interrogated.

The wind increased, sweeping through the wall and swirling around him, lifting his own stench to his nose. He gagged at the moist, noxious scent of blood and sweat he'd been living with for months. The wind had a way of balling it up and delivering it anew like a putrefied appetizer.

He began to shiver. To stay warm, he had to start moving. Reluctantly, he pushed away from the bars and resumed his pacing, striving to keep his arm stable to minimize cascades of pain.

Days in the cell. Tedious. A puzzle, Dearborn's visit on the previous night. His hanging face, his air of resignation. He lacked altogether the comportment of a soldier. Baxter had expected more regality.

Nothing can be predicted about people, Baxter thought. Who would have guessed me capable of what I've done? Before, the idea would have sounded like lunacy. Cannot expect otherwise from others. Cannot doubt anyone's capacity for change.

Quite long enough, though the wait was not surprising. Proper procedures would have to be followed. Dearborn consults the governor, who in turn consults the president. In the end nothing would be written down. Will they dig a hole for me specifically or shovel me under with the rest? Maybe for punishment I'll be left for the ravens and coyotes. The latter sounded agreeable. He'd spent enough time underground.

Incomprehensible that he felt no despair. He remembered feeling it, and he shuddered, thinking, I will not survive another episode. I am too weak now.

Boredom: the enemy. Stasis, too. While he had been able to act, commitment kept him from despair. Steps needed to be completed. Tasks awaited attention. Rest was a disease to be cured with work. He thought, Justice is a victor's word. Since I am the last witness, I will claim it. The word, no longer a vapor to me. Goodbye, cloud. Goodbye, mist. I saw and see through you. With nothing left to love, one thinks of revenge and death. One works to collapse in pursuit of them. When Dearborn took away his hate, he would be sorry to feel it go.

No matter how long it takes, no stopping now. It will play out to the end. How smoothly the machine purrs on. Clean the sand from the bearings, restart the mechanism. Had their actions made any impact? He stopped at that question. The answer did not matter.

He smiled weakly. Hawkins.

Pace and move. Endure the pain. He felt some heat beneath his clothes.

5

Distraction plagued him the following day as he walked with Thomas and Lorraine to the commissary. He could not disengage his mind from work. A degree of hesitation on Lind's part was justified given safety considerations. Nothing could be worse for him than for his boss to die on his watch. But Baxter would not allow a subordinate, however well-intentioned, to impede him. He had to familiarize himself with unfamiliar surroundings. Otherwise, he might never know what was being concealed from him. Lind had been notified in advance of his arrival, so hazards or deficiencies might already have been covered up. At the same time it seemed impossible that what he'd experienced on his sole shift had been in any way sanitized. God help them if it's really worse than what I went through, he thought.

"We're here," Thomas said, and the small hand which Baxter had been holding dropped away. The boy scurried through the screen door, and Lorraine said, "Don't run!" as it slammed behind him.

"He's happy to be away from the house," Baxter said. He did not remember the walk.

"Welcome back to the land of the sentient," Lorraine said.

The clerk was a blonde of around sixteen. He greeted them at first with nothing more than an indifferent glance, but when he recognized his customers, he straightened up with a confected smile. Baxter found the about-face undignified.

"Can I help you folks with anything?"

Offering a scrap of paper, Lorraine said, "I made a list."

He hurried from behind the counter. "Let me find those things for you, ma'am." With Lorraine trailing him, he navigated the aisles with the efficiency of a well-practiced page.

Baxter wandered about the shelves. He did not know what to make of Lind's participation in Homestead. An experience like that could warp a man's judgment.

Bad management had caused Homestead, nothing more. Carnegie, away in Europe, leaves Frick in charge, who slashes wages to break a union drive, which precipitates a strike, which necessitates the hiring of guards, Lind apparently among them, to protect the strikebreakers. And it was not true that none of the organizers were punished. Berkman, the anarchist leader, got fourteen years. Homestead didn't have to unfold the way it did. Frick made colossally bad decisions. He could have offered concessions short of unionization. Token things. Wage cuts were a blatant provocation. Lind's I-was-there argument struck Baxter as absurd. Experience could be valuable, but it wasn't omniscience.

Thomas came to him, two licorice whips in hand. "Can I buy these?"

"With what?"

Thomas sighed dramatically. "Can *you* buy them for me?"

"I'll ask your mother." Baxter picked up a can of milk from the shelf. The price seemed exorbitant, but he rarely did the shopping. "Does it cost this much at home?" he asked Lorraine.

She examined the tag. "In Brooklyn it's about half this, but that's the way it is with everything here." She held up a sack of coffee. "Twice what it costs in New York. If we actually had to pay, you'd need a second job."

Baxter approached the clerk. "Who sets the prices?"

"Prices don't matter for you," the boy said. "You've got a blank check."

"That's not what I asked."

"Oh. I'm not really sure. I get a price sheet every month from Mr. Lind, but I don't think he makes it up. I think he just delivers it."

"Why is everything so expensive?"

"I don't know. Shipping, maybe?"

Baxter thought for a moment. "Mark everything down by a third."

"Sir?"

"I trust you know how to do the mathematics."

"Yes, sir. But it's just, I don't think I should do that, sir. I'll get in a lot of trouble."

"Just say I told you to."

The clerk noted their purchases, including the licorice, and loaded them into paper sacks. Gathering the groceries into his arms, Baxter said to the clerk, "I'm not going to come back tomorrow and see that nothing has changed, am I?"

"No, sir. One third. I promise."

~

With Lind, Baxter toured the property for days. As promised, Baxter was taken everywhere he asked to go, although he did not press for access again to the stopes. When he told Lind of the price reductions at the commissary, Lind delayed and clenched his jaw before saying only, "Yes, sir." Baxter had no problem antagonizing Lind if he felt it was necessary, but he wasn't looking to irritate him for the sole purpose of reminding him of his place.

Another week sufficed for Baxter to familiarize himself with the filing and accounting systems in the office. If he later wanted access to pay scales or accident rates, he would be able to find them without bothering Lind.

Baxter took yet another week to draft his report. He wrote at the house, which was quieter and more peaceful than the office and, so long as he stayed out of town, he was not interrupted. Lind was instructed not to disturb him unless absolutely necessary. Baxter wrote with difficulty, as always, not that he was intimidated by the task. He was simply intent on making his meaning clear, troublesome enough under ordinary circumstances, more so in consequential documents. At least his hands had not suppurated. They were not yet fully healed, but they were on the mend. He persevered.

When he finished the report, he admitted to himself that all the trouble of his transfer had probably not been necessary. The report struck him as unremarkable, his recommendations banal. Among them: the scales should be properly calibrated, to which end the company's weighman should be complemented by a miner elected by his peers to provide independent verification; the tonnage rates should be slightly hiked; a flat weekly supplement should be instituted for dead work.

For the present, the company might be wise to hold in reserve one or another of these improvements so as to offer it later to de-escalate a union drive. If the men would not settle, the company could offer more and more, dreaming up incentives as need be. In Baxter's view, the company ought to do what it could to inspire goodwill. The remedying of simple grievances cost next to nothing. He also included Mr. Lind's categorical objections to any and all concessions.

It was late afternoon when Baxter signed his final draft and bound it for mailing. He relaxed on the porch while Lorraine prepared dinner. Less than a month had passed since his arrival, but daytime heat was already forsaking the valley. He looked at the horizon and the bleached hues of the land. Here, at some distance from town, the air in the evening cooled with transitory autumn, smelling frangible and clean. He felt a twinge of ambivalence about the end of his term. He had grown to enjoy the quiet and calm of the desert, so different from the city. His dress had grown more casual in Colorado, too. He was not particularly excited about donning a daily suit again.

At least under his watch a strike had been avoided. He did not specifically know why. Perhaps the union couldn't bankroll a stoppage. Perhaps the men needed their wages too badly in the short term. Baxter satisfied himself with the knowledge that his report was solid, succinct, objective, and impersonal, and he looked forward to the stories of the west he'd now be able to tell over cigars and brandy.

He thought back to the day before he'd worked his first and only shift. Lind took him into a mainline tunnel where the surface light gave way to a string of tiny electric bulbs along the timber shoring of the roof. A sickly yellow glow illuminated the track and pipes on the floor. Baxter stumbled and stopped. The tunnel was warm, much warmer than the surface. Drops of sweat slid down his back. He wiped his forehead and looked around. "Coal in its natural state. I've never seen it before."

"This is more of a transfer room. The men bring the coal here from other stopes and load it onto larger carts. Farther up, some of those carts get dumped on the conveyors. The rest come out by mule."

Baxter walked his gaze across the ceiling. Much of the shoring was visibly decrepit—timbers pocked with rot, splinters hanging like hairs from the wood. "The supports look weak."

Lind kicked absentmindedly at the track. "Just looking at those timbers doesn't tell you much. The top surface may be chewed up, but as long as the wood underneath is solid, there's no problem. Anyhow, wops are cheaper than props."

Let that pass, Baxter thought. "I'd like to see where the coal comes from."

"Can we do that another day? Next shift will be coming on soon. Probably not wise for us to be mucking around in here with the men trying to work."

Lind's first dodge. Baxter had not recognized it at the time. He remembered why. He had not eaten that morning. A chance for a break appealed to him. A hollowed-out stomach had clouded him.

He felt low with shame at how he'd allowed himself to be led. His first visit to the supply shop. Fifteen men lined up for gear. Behind the counter, a dark-haired man in his fifties with a withered arm.

"This here's Nikos. Been our supply clerk for a while. He was injured about ten years back, so I made him a gear jockey."

Plodding, the men inched forward. Forlorn in their denim jackets, overalls, and shabby leather boots, they moved past the two bosses to the counter. The gear clinked and knocked together. Picks and shovels, pads of scrap rubber, rolls of wax paper, brass tags to designate loads, black powder, hanks of fuse, electric headlamps. The men gathered it all into armfuls and did their best to exit without fumbling.

Outside, more spectacle. At the larger driftmouths, conveyor belts heavy with material crawled out of the darkness and into a tiered system of wooden troughs. Young boys sat by, picking over the belts. Filthy as bilge rats, the boys wore tams and tattered jackets, some only shirtsleeves. Here was a spine crooked at a severe angle, there was a right hand hanging useless, crushed flat. A few of the boys appeared to be Thomas' age, and none of them looked older than fourteen.

"These boys," Baxter said. "What's their purpose?"

"Breaker boys. They sort the coal from the slate. They do a standard shift. Twelve hours."

Baxter pinched the bridge of his nose against a headache that grew and grew.

6

"Dad?"

Baxter porpoised momentarily into consciousness.

"Dad."

He felt something on his shoulder.

"Mom?"

A hand. A boy's hand. "Thomas," Baxter said in a half whisper. He snapped awake and sat upright. "What's wrong?"

"The house is shaking."

Baxter squeezed the sleep from his eyes. "What?"

Lorraine woke. "Thomas, what is it?"

"The house is shaking. It woke me up."

"You must have dreamed it, sweetheart."

"Maybe not," Baxter said, trying to think. "They could be blasting."

"In the middle of the night?"

"I don't know. It's possible."

Then he felt it. The house shivered as if with fever. He heard a distant thudding.

"See?" Thomas said.

"It's nothing to worry about. They're just blowing some coal out of the ground," Baxter said. "How many thumps did you feel before you came in here?"

Thomas thought for a moment. "Four."

"Including that last one?"

"Five."

Maybe too many, maybe not, Baxter thought. He rose from bed, searching for his slippers. "It's late. Try to go back to sleep, son."

"I'm scared."

"Would it make you feel better to sleep with us tonight?" Lorraine asked.

Thomas nodded and curled into the already warm bed. Baxter covered his son with the blanket and headed for the door.

Lorraine said, "Where are you going?"

"Just to have a look."

The house frissoned again, much more gently this time, and as he stepped onto the porch, he saw only the desert as it had lain since their arrival. Another blast came. This time he looked toward town.

He cursed and ran inside, searching desperately for his shoes.

~

He had no trouble finding his way. The night flashed with horrid orange fire. At the driftmouth by the clapboard post office, Lind and a passel of guards surrounded the mine entrance, pounding back the off-shift miners who had fallen upon them. The guards swung away as more men poured in from town and the bluffside shacks.

"Get back!" Lind screamed. He smashed about with his rifle butt, and a man fell down with his face masked in blood. "Get back, goddammit!"

Baxter ran toward Lind, yelling, "What happened? What's going on?"

"Get out of here!" Lind shouted back at him.

The shaft exhaled a boom and a whoosh, and a shock wave slammed across the entire ventral surface of Baxter's body. He had barely enough time to realize he was airborne before he crashed to the ground again, his injured torso detonating with pain. All around, clumps of dirt rained down with splintered timbers and rock. Baxter rolled onto his stomach and covered his head. He tried to cry out but could not, the impact having robbed him of breath.

Tendrils of fire licked the roof of the driftmouth and withdrew. The windows of the post office had been shattered. Baxter's hands worked uselessly at the dirt, clutching and unclutching until he regained his wind with gulping, savage gasps.

The blast had shaved many of the men to the ground, and as they regained their feet, Baxter heard Chamm's voice calling out, "Enough! *Eparkis!*"

Lind coughed, "Keep your men in line."

A miner started for Lind, but Chamm barked, "*Basta, basta!*" The miner checked his advance. Then, so did the others. They fell back shouting intermittently, menacingly restive as fire crackled from within the mine.

"We'll go in from the north side and check it out," Chamm said to Lind.

Lind's eyes stayed locked on the crowd of miners. "You don't call the shots around here."

"You saw that last rip. She's blown herself out, most likely."

Lind aimed his weapon at Chamm's face. "We'll follow procedure like we always do. Back off."

Chamm moved away. He ground his teeth, then noticed Baxter alone in the dirt beside the main mass of standing men.

"What you think on it, boss man?"

Baxter staggered to his feet, bent over in pain, a hand covering where his side had met the ground. He spat the pieces of a tooth from his mouth. Chamm came to him and put an arm around him, ostensibly for assistance. He squeezed hard on Baxter's ribs. Baxter yelped and fell to one knee.

"Got yourself a knot there, huh?" Chamm said. "You're a miner now, ain't you?"

"Shut up," Lind said.

Chamm wheeled on him. "Last time I heard, this man's your boss. I wager he's got more say than you do."

"He's got nothing to say, not about this."

"That right, Baxter? You gonna let your head thug run the show?"

Baxter could not think. He slumped, breathing hard.

"Some miner you are." Chamm spat. "Look here," he said to Lind. "You don't let us do what we can, we'll dump the water on the whole operation."

Sweating, Lind panted, "You can check the north mainway if you want."

Chamm tore off with the other men following.

"Stay out of the stopes!" Lind called after them. "I don't care if they look clear!"

"What now?" Baxter said with hitched breaths.

"Come on," Lind said. He threaded a hand into Baxter's armpit and helped him straighten up.

~

At the doctor's office, Baxter could not climb fully onto the examination table, so he merely leaned against it as Lind watched from the door.

"Raise up your shirt," the doctor said. He squinted at the wound. "This here's already starting to purple. You hurt it before?"

"In the mine," Baxter said.

"You told me it was nothing," Lind said.

"It was, until now."

The doctor touched the bruise. Baxter twitched in pain.

"Not too bad," the doctor said.

"Broken?" Lind asked.

"Don't think so." The doctor lit a cigarette. "I can tape it up for you if you want."

"Will that help?" Baxter asked.

The doctor shrugged. "Can't hurt." He fetched tape from a nearby drawer and slapped on successive strips. Baxter's eyes watered with the pain of each pressing.

"Has to be tight," the doctor said. "Otherwise there's no support."

"I'll bet you see a lot of injuries like this," Baxter said.

The doctor stopped for a moment. He looked at Lind. "He's got a right smart sense of humor, doesn't he?"

Baxter said, "What's so funny?"

"Don't worry about it," the doctor said, continuing with the taping.

Baxter pushed the doctor's hands away and flared, "Somebody better give me a straight answer. I'm in no mood to be toyed with."

"Easy, easy," Lind said. "He didn't mean anything. There's a charge for the doctor, so folks here tend to use him only when really necessary. Not too many miners come in over something like a bruise."

Baxter turned to the doctor. "Doesn't the company deduct your salary from the overall scrip?"

"Sure," the doctor said, pressing a final piece of tape into place. "But that's my retainer. Individual services have to be paid for individually. Usually I see folks when they need something chopped off or sewn up."

Baxter lowered his shirt over the patch. "Do you think that's fair?"

"I never thought much about it," the doctor said. "I don't make the rules, I just follow them." He stubbed out his cigarette on the side of the examination table.

"Leave us alone for a minute," Lind said to the doctor.

The doctor walked into the next room, and Lind sat down on a stool beside the examination table. "He's got a hell of a nerve," Baxter said as he struggled to tuck in his shirt.

"He don't like to be told his business, just like you don't like to be told yours."

"What do we do now?"

"First step is to see how bad the situation is, whether the fire's still spreading."

"Chamm said it might have blown itself out."

"There's a chance of that. Not a good one, but we'll see."

"And you allowed them to go in by themselves?"

"The miners? If they want to risk their necks for a look around, they can, within reason. That's procedure, as long as they stay in the mainway. Who knows those tunnels better? If there's a fire in the stopes, they won't be able to get in anyway. Too hot, too small. Might have to seal off the mainway to cut the oxygen, though. When there's a fire, a tunnel can act like a chimney. Don't worry. My boys will handle everything, corral the men if they get too antsy."

"How long until all of this is sorted out?"

"Could be a few days," Lind said. "Maybe longer. Hard to tell. You want me to wire Mr. Robertson?"

"I'll write out something for a telegram. It's better if he hears it from me."

"You need help getting home?"

"No. Go, go. Keep me posted."

Lind hurried off, and Baxter tried to find a tolerable depth of breathing. He knew that despite his injury he should have followed Lind and lent a hand, yet he could not bring himself to do anything but limp home, thinking only of his pain.

Dearborn lowered him to the floor so as not to shock his arm, saying, "Easy now," coaxing, gentle.

The cell door closed. Baxter could not see anything. His eyes clamped shut with paroxysms of pain. Movement had broken the brick-like stiffness that had settled into his body. His breath heaved as if he were hauling rocks. He fought to remain conscious. After a few minutes of motionlessness, an intense but attritable ache returned.

"You all right?" Dearborn asked.

An exhale from Baxter, devoid of words.

"All right, then." From his breast pocket Dearborn withdrew cigarettes. He offered Baxter first-smoke and was rebuffed. Dearborn lit up. "I hear you're from New York."

"I live in Brooklyn."

"And you work—pardon me, worked—on Wall Street. That's quite a change. This is the first time I've been to Colorado. I enjoyed the ride, although I wish we were meeting under better circumstances."

"The ride?" Baxter coughed once, winced, and spat with difficulty. "It's nothing but desert."

"What's wrong with that? We haven't sullied it yet."

"It's barren."

"Oh, I don't know. If we spent more time here, I think we'd come to see it as alive as anywhere else."

"I used to know a man whose sole wish was to go back to his forest, his hills."

"I'd like to meet him someday."

"He's dead now."

"Unfortunate." Dearborn looked at the floor and then moved to the hole in the wall, watching the plain. "All right."

"How long am I going to be here?"

"Hard to say. We'll have a look around. Depending on what we find, we'll wire back, get proper instructions." From the end of his cigarette Dearborn tapped a cylinder of ash which fell and exploded on the floor. "Care to say what we'll find out there?"

"I already told you." Shifting to a new position, Baxter grunted and subsided.

"Nothing."

"That's right."

"You're the last one."

"Right."

Dearborn squatted near the bars. "I've got no malice toward any man, Baxter. I'm beyond all that. Do you believe me?"

7

Baxter stirred little from bed for the next three days, and Lind visited him only at the close of the second. Holding his hat before him, Lind filled the space of the bedroom jamb. Baxter waved him in.

"Report, please," Baxter said.

"You're not going to like it."

"Bad news first."

"Five men dead."

Baxter closed his eyes and sunk away for a moment. "And the good news?"

"Same as the bad. Five men dead. *Only* five. That's how many were still inside when we sealed it up."

Baxter went cold, hoping he had not heard correctly. "When you sealed what up?"

"The mainway."

"You said you would only seal that tunnel if you had to."

"And I had to."

"But that's where Chamm and his men were."

"We cleared them out first. The ones that were trapped were farther down in. Unreachable. Chamm will tell you different, but he's wrong. There was no chance we could have gotten to those other boys."

"You took two days to tell me all of this? You couldn't have sent a runner with a note?"

"With all due respect, Mr. Baxter, I'm trying to run a mine here. Those men are dead, and dead is dead. I figured it was more important to keep a lid on the town before I worried about anything else.

Between his fingers Baxter held a portion of the sheet, hot now from rubbing. "We were going to follow procedure."

"To the letter."

"Procedure is to abandon men to their deaths?"

"Procedure is to mine and sell coal."

"Don't be flippant. There are priorities."

"That's right," Lind said. "First, coal. Second, equipment. Third, mules. Fourth, men."

"You should have tried to save them."

"We did, but that shaft was the main oxygen source for the fire. If we'd left it open for a few more hours, it would have meant more tunnels burned out, more timbers charred, more walls and ceilings brittled. Cart tracks? Every one of them warped by heat would have to be replaced, which means lost productivity, lost jobs. Or we could leave them as-is, and then you could start tallying up the men killed by derailments. We sealed the shaft and got lucky. The fire didn't spread. Looks like it burned itself out in less than an hour. Sure the miners are going to argue, but they don't have to make the decisions. We do. And what we did will save more lives than it took."

Baxter felt a little sick. "Do you know what caused the explosion?"

"Can't rule out sabotage."

"Excuse me?"

"Happens from time to time."

"Why would miners blow themselves up?"

"No better rally cry for a union."

Baxter scoffed. "And you think that's plausible?"

"Probably not this time, but it's impossible to know for sure. The fire would have burned off the evidence. And it probably wasn't methane. We shut the tunnels with buildups of that years ago. My guess is dust."

"What kind of dust?"

"Coal, slate, sandstone. One kind of dust is as good as another. You grind down anything fine enough and sooner or later it torches up."

"We should wet the shafts down more thoroughly."

"Mr. Baxter, look at what's happening with those slag heaps at the tipple. You saw them. You walked right past them when you came for weigh-in with Chamm. They're mountains of slate and low-grade coal. The chemistry in the mix causes spontaneous combustion. They're burning from the inside out, all the time, day and night, and every day we're dumping more fuel on them. Where'd you think all the black smoke comes from? Most of the time, the wind pushes it north over the plain, but every so often it turns and comes to town. When that happens, there's an oily black coating on everything— people, buildings, you name it. I've seen it take the paint right off the walls. Now, rain ain't going to put out those slag-heap fires, and don't you think if I had the water I'd try to do something about them? All I can do is send a few men out from time to time to cover a fireline with dirt or cinders, scratch out a trench if a fire looks to spread. That's it. Slag-heap fires are part of mining, just like dust is. This is a desert. We do our best, but there's never enough water to go around."

Baxter felt the need to leave the room, pull different air into his lungs. "We're shutting operations temporarily."

"Sir?"

"The least we can do is give them time to mourn their dead."

"A memorial period," Lind said. He clicked his teeth together. "Yes, I guess we could do that."

Baxter inched to the edge of the bed until he could swing his legs down and feel the floor beneath his feet. With Lind's help, he stood up, wobbling precipitately. "Tell your men to review their water us-age. I want any surplus they can dredge up reallocated to alleviating the dust."

63

"Yes, sir."

"Nothing else, I take it?" Baxter said. He moved painfully to the door. He supported himself with one hand on the jamb.

"Just one thing."

It was not difficult to guess. "A strike."

"You can practically bet on it."

He sent Lind away. Beyond what he'd already ordered, Baxter floundered for what to do about the situation. He focused therefore on a minor but essential task. A note would have to be added to his report. The old man would have to be informed of the deaths and of Baxter's willingness to see out their consequences. As for what he'd previously written, Baxter didn't think there was reason to change it. He still believed in the recommendations. He opened the bedside table for pen, ink, and some paper, cognizant that a strike would delay a homecoming. For how long, there was no telling.

~

Baxter came downstairs, holding the handrail to minimize his movements. At the stove, he prepared kindling and water for coffee. The noise of the iron burner rattling into its seat brought Lorraine to him.

"Why didn't you call me? I would have done this for you."

"I'm sore, not crippled," Baxter said. He settled into a chair at the table. A short time ago it had been his routine to rise in Brooklyn at six-thirty, catch the seven-fifteen to Manhattan, and be behind his desk before the market opened. Now, half a continent away, preparing coffee on a wood-fired stove had become just another task he barely had to think about to accomplish. He smiled wanly despite his worries.

"Penny for your thoughts," Lorraine said.

"'Man is the creature that can get used to anything.' Dostoyevsky, I think."

"Yes, well, you've done quite enough testing of your limits. The last thing I need is a dead husband."

The lid of the pot clattered as the water boiled. Lorraine scooped in some coffee grounds.

"Later today I'm going into town," he said.

"You most certainly are not. You can barely make it down the stairs. You need to rest."

"I have to mail the report. I also have to survey the damage, at least put in an appearance. There are men a lot worse off than I am after that explosion."

"How many were injured?" she asked, pouring the coffee.

"Five men were killed in the fire. That's what Lind was here to talk to me about."

"Dear God . . ."

"They were trapped in the stope when the explosion occurred, and then the mainway had to be closed. There was no way to rescue them. That's my understanding."

"Lind closed the tunnel with the men still inside? How could you allow that?"

"I wasn't there, if you recall. And in any case I didn't know Lind was going to do it. He didn't know he was going to do it. It's a complicated problem. There are perfectly arguable reasons for what he did. A fire does a lot of damage. There are safety issues to consider. The only way to prevent the fire from spreading was to seal the tunnel, cut off its oxygen source." He resented that she'd guilted him into an explanation. He didn't think he had anything to confess. The decision had not been his. Lind had made it in the course of events. Repeating Lind's analysis didn't mean he agreed with it. He was still turning it over in his mind. The small, thin figure of Thomas distracted him. The boy had appeared in the doorway, watching with curiosity.

"You're better," Thomas said.

"A little," Baxter said. "I have to go into town today for a while, so I want you to behave for your mother."

"What are you going to hurt next?"

"Nothing, I hope," Baxter chuckled, "but I haven't been having the best of luck lately."

Abruptly, Thomas left the kitchen, and Baxter could hear the sound of hurried rummaging in the next room. He set his coffee down and in the parlor found Thomas submerged in the chest of toys they'd brought along from New York. When he surfaced, he handed his father a rabbit's foot.

~

Report in hand, Baxter made his painstaking way toward town and to the shaft near the post office. The postman, outside on a ladder, was helping another man repair the windows and patch the damaged building with scrap wood. Flames had darkened the rock walls of the shaft. The postman came down from the ladder. He was a short man with a potbelly and shoulders thrust forward.

"I know you have a lot on your hands right now," Baxter said, holding out the report, "but is there any way you can post this to New York?"

"I'll put it in with today's load."

In town, Baxter was struck by the air of normalcy. Shifts turned. Maybe Lind had not yet announced the suspension of operations. More perplexing was the lack of protest and upheaval. The men in the streets did not appear particularly agitated. They walked about with the same comportment of depletion he'd observed since his arrival. When Lind used the word "strike" Baxter had prepared himself for something out of Steffens or Sinclair, but maybe their critics were right. Maybe they were just lying publicity hounds.

The mainway was no longer sealed. Planking and four rolls of canvas, the remains of the cap that had been erected across the tunnel, lay in stacks about its mouth. The ventilation fan on the ceiling was running in reverse to draw out residual smoke and gas, and a pair of guards were loading the seal materials onto a mule-driven cart to be hauled away.

Saying nothing, the guards looked at each other and then at Baxter.

"Is it safe to go inside?" Baxter asked.

"Not too far, I guess. Ain't gonna see much. The bodies—what was left of them, leastways—already been pulled out."

Baxter tried to step into the tunnel. Instead he stood looking into it to where the light failed and defeated his eyes. Something thumped him and splattered. Startled, sulphur fumes rose into his nose as he picked the remains of a rotten egg from his sleeve. The woman who'd thrown it had stolen up on him. "Have you lost your mind?" he said.

"Listen to that!" She wore a beige gingham dress with a full-length apron. Both garments were heavily patched with mismatched material. Her oil-black hair stood in sharp contrast to her pale skin and clothes. Her face was plain with a flat nose supporting spectacles above a thin, expressive mouth. "Ain't you got a nerve, showin' your face," she said.

She appeared to be around forty, and she came toward him so quickly that he thought she would knock him over. He took a step back, and she stopped.

"I ain't afraid of you. You want to arrest me, go ahead. I've seen a hell of a lot worse than the inside of a jailhouse. What you going to do to us that's worse than working for your company? Nothing. But we ain't standing by to watch you burn up our men."

"Madam, I cannot express how sorry I am about what happened. Everything possible was done to save them."

"Who told you that?"

"Mr. Lind."

"You believe that pussel-gutted hog?"

"I'm sorry, ma'am. I wasn't here at the time. I was on the other side of town. I was injured at the initial explosion. I didn't see what happened later."

"Ain't that convenient."

He squeezed his eyes, mustering patience. "What is your name?"

"Anna Chamm. You jerked my husband around in the mine the other day."

Baxter stopped cleaning himself and wilted a little. "He helped me a lot. I'm sorry if he felt ill-used."

She ceased speaking, and, lost for appropriate words, Baxter opted for the observable. "Work is continuing."

"Why shouldn't it? We gotta eat."

"Yes, but Mr. Lind was supposed to inform you of a mourning period."

"He did. Nobody believed him."

"I assure you it's true. Part of the reason I came to town was to see that it went smoothly. Otherwise I would still be in bed."

The anger in her face transformed into puzzlement. Without another word, she turned from him and walked away. Feeling wrung out, Baxter tossed his now ruined jacket to the ground and went to find Lind.

"*That must be something.*"

"*Worst thing in the world,*" Dearborn said. "*Makes you feel all dead and cold inside. Makes you lonesome. Love will cure it, but sometimes love doesn't come along in time. Don't you agree?*"

"*Everyone I love is dead, but I don't hate anyone.*"

"*The first part might be true, but the second part isn't. Only hate makes a mess like the one outside.*"

"*I didn't do it alone.*"

"*But you're alone now. At least that's what you'd have me believe.*"

"*I told you the truth. I have no reason to lie.*"

"*You had one before?*" Dearborn ground out the nub of his cigarette. "*Don't worry. I believe you. Of course it would make no difference if I didn't. We'd search regardless. My men would be just as careful. The facts will win the day. And keep your hate. That's something worth holding on to. Love can make you feel alive, but so can hate.*"

"*And you say you have none left.*"

"*I would give anything to get it back.*"

"*Even your life?*"

"*Without half a thought.*"

"*Then you wouldn't be around to enjoy it.*"

"*No.*"

"*That makes no sense.*"

"I guess it doesn't. Score one for you, Baxter. Would you like something to read?"

A book? Jailed by a lunatic. At least a calm one. Plausible also that Dearborn was needling him. Baxter knew the question that would tell immediately. He held it in reserve.

"I used to love to read," Dearborn said. "I would read for hours and hours. I don't do that anymore. I wish I could say it's because I don't have the time, but I do. Something pulls you to books when you're young. Less so later. Melville was my scripture. Have you read him?"

"Once when I was twelve. I suppose you're going to compare me to Ahab now."

"Oh, no," Dearborn said. "Not in the least. Pip is your name. You're out of the boat, left behind."

"You're memory is faulty," Baxter said. "Pip is from Dickens, not Melville."

Dearborn clucked his tongue. "Trust me. You jumped to save your life. That's rarely forgiven. They're already cursing you."

Too many questions, too much discussion.

"Leave me alone, please."

"Certainly," Dearborn said. He left.

Remarkable.

8

Feet brushed softly along the dirt, and everyone who had not chosen to join the lines watched from the porches and steps of Main Street. The men walked hatless and scrubbed, the women matching them in their finest dark clothes. Baxter had not seen the employees so presentable before, and it was sobering to witness their decorum. Had this been New York, the police would have outnumbered the mourners just to keep the traffic away and the procession moving smoothly. Lind's men were on hand, but they hung in the alleys between buildings, obeying Baxter's orders to remain at a distance.

Two parallel lines trailed the bearers of the cheap, scrap-wood coffins. From the front, two men beat time on drums with muffled heads. Clouds didn't combat the sun, and as they passed, the men's faces were slick with sweat and respect, carrying expressions of somber importance. Far beyond the mourners, from the stack of the tipple's generator, a curl of black smoke beckoned to the sky. The lines lifted black and red flags, held but not waved, and beneath them rose the occasional sound of choked tears from angry eyes. The coffins, high on their bearers' shoulders, moved like a small convoy of ships on a calm sea.

Baxter, his family beside him, bowed his head and waited. Lind came to him to speak, but Baxter cut him short with a slice of his hand. Lind was still wearing his hat. Baxter said, "Show some respect, for Christ's sake." The hat was removed, but without sufficient alacrity.

Nearly an hour passed before the entire procession cleared the town and snaked to the cemetery on the plain. Baxter was relieved to have the ceremony closed without incident. Drained, he and his family made their way to the house, quiet with lingering melancholy. Baxter sat with Lorraine and Thomas in the parlor.

"Were those men old?" Thomas asked.

"No, son. They were all around twenty-five."

"Did it hurt when they died?"

Baxter imagined the men choking on black smoke, clawing at the back side of the seal for escape, their minds reeling with panic. Of course it might have been more basic than that. They might simply have burned to death. "I don't think so."

Lorraine pulled Thomas into her lap. "Try not to think about it."

"That's right," Baxter said. "Try to put it out of your mind."

The boy's face rumpled with frustration. He knew that information was being withheld from him, but he couldn't articulate the grievance. That was just fine with Baxter. He wasn't going to be goaded into spilling the actualities.

"Why don't you pick out a book?" Lorraine said. "I'll fetch you some milk. We'll read for a while together."

Sullenly, the boy climbed down from her lap and left the room. Baxter followed his wife into the kitchen where he poured himself a whiskey. "I hope I never see anything like that again."

"It's probably the most time off they've ever had," Lorraine said.

"What's done is done. I never said Lind made the right decision. I only said there was an argument for it. Don't blame me for things I didn't do."

She walked away in search of Thomas. Baxter swore in a whisper. He carried his drink to the porch. Did she think the awfulness was lost on him? Maybe not, but awfulness alone explains nothing. Lots of things are awful. The question is what to do about them. Stewing, he sat on the porch for a time, but before he had finished his drink, a man approached the house. He stopped as Baxter waved to him, then continued forward again uncertainly. "Mr. Chamm," Baxter said, offering his hand. Chamm reciprocated, but had trouble looking Baxter in the eye.

"What can I do for you?" Baxter asked. In keeping with the day, he tried to speak kindly. Chamm had still not said a word, so Baxter conducted him onto the porch. Gesturing toward the wicker chairs, he said, "Please," and they both sat down, Chamm only on the edge of the chair.

"Can I get you a drink?"

"No, thank you," Chamm said. He kneaded the calluses of his right hand. His eyes sat deep and red in their sockets. "We appreciate the time to get our folks put proper in the ground. We thought someone should come out and say something. It's been a long time since the company showed us any courtesy."

"It was the least we could do," Baxter said. "Did you know the men who were killed?"

"Sure," Chamm said, "but I wouldn't call 'em kin. Still, dead ain't no good for anybody." His gaze stayed on the planks of the porch.

Baxter set his drink down and leaned forward, opening his hands. "You don't have to walk on eggshells with me. And for what it's worth, you don't strike me as a timid sort."

"I didn't have to thank you for nothin' before."

"Mr. Lind told me dust was probably to blame for the accident."

"Looks that way."

"If you think something else caused the explosion, please tell me. I want to know the truth. It's important that I know so I can stop this from happening again, or at least try."

"Dust is our guess, too. Lind probably has that one straight."

"But not the sealing of the tunnel."

"We didn't see it the way he did. Nothing to do about it now."

With attempted lightness, Baxter said, "I met your wife yesterday."

"Yes, sir. She mentioned that. I should apologize for her."

"No need to apologize, but I must say, I've had better introductions."

"Don't hold her no grudge if you can. She's just a little tempered. She keeps me and my boy in line pretty good."

"You have a son?"

"Yes, sir. Name of Oliver."

"How old?"

"About eight now. This valley ain't no place to raise a little one."

Feeling his misstep, Baxter cleared his throat and emptied his drink. He peered into the barren glass. "Are you sure you wouldn't like a drink?"

"Yes, sir. I'm sure. I'm a teetotaler, matter of fact. Comin' up in the hollers, I seen the damage liquor can do. I like to keep sharp, and that stuff dulls you round as a pebble."

That's why I drink it, Baxter thought. He said, "When I was with you in the mine, did you recognize me? Did anyone?"

"We knew something was off. You'd only been around a day or so. Nobody got a good enough look at you to be sure, leastways not out of your suit. New folks come in from time to time and Lind don't say nothing about 'em so we figured on even chances you were company versus working man. Fact that you might not have spoke English or couldn't hear or speak don't mean much. Lind's hired ragged gear before. Most times it's best just to see how a man works. Shut your trap and wait. Things naked themselves up after a while. It always works like that. Just got to give it time."

"How did I hold up?"

"Tolerable. Clumsy though. I kept an eye on you so you didn't hurt yourself too bad. You never know how Lind will play it if somebody comes out busted up. Usually he don't notice." Chamm opened his mouth as if to continue, but then he closed it again.

"What about when he does notice?" Baxter prodded.

"He yelps about safety and somebody gets an unpaid shift for pun-ishment. Usually that shitstorm empties on my head."

"Why you?"

Chamm shrugged.

Baxter studied him. Eustas Chamm, portrait of closure. The shoulders concave, the back hunched, protective. Baxter didn't want to jeopardize whatever headway he'd made by pushing for details on a strike. The day would not support small-scale brinksmanship. Chamm would most likely claim ignorance anyway. "I'm glad you came to see me," Baxter said, standing. "Thank you again. The com-pany will do its best to see there are no more accidents."

Rising, too, Chamm said, "Forgive me, sir, but we've heard that before."

"I imagine it's not very reassuring."

"It's just that folks get tired a livin' on talk."

"I'm going to do my best while I'm in the valley," Baxter said. "I'm afraid my word is all you have to go on at this point."

They shook hands, and this time Baxter felt less trepidation in Chamm's grip. Chamm began the walk back toward town, and Bax-ter stepped off the porch to watch him go. To the east on the plain, two small silhouettes were rounding off the tops of fresh graves.

Dearborn brought him food. After so long in the tunnels, Baxter had forgotten the taste of actual meals. His stomach had shrunk from surviving on lentils and water. Five months in the tunnels, he thought. Five months. We were moles.

Dearborn also brought him blankets and talk. Both helped. He was still cold, but he had stopped shivering. Cold the night before. Death near at hand. He asked for help even though he had not wanted to, had not wanted to relinquish himself. He felt he could last longer.

He had clunked a scrap of wood against the bars. They rang dully from the impacts. Impossible that this bit of motion could drain him of energy as much as it did. He leaned on the bars, recovering his breath. A soldier appeared in the room. Baxter did not recognize him. He looked the same as all the others.

"We ain't supposed to come in here," the soldier said.

"Dearborn."

"I ain't Dearborn, you stupid red."

"Get him for me. I want to talk to him."

The soldier exited, and Baxter drew up on the bed frame. How much time passed before Dearborn entered, Baxter could not say. Too long. Dearborn saw him shivering and hurried off again, returning with more blankets.

The wool raked against Baxter's skin, scratching through its shell of grime. The blankets were sufficient to block the wind. Immediately he felt warmer. For some minutes he curled into the wool, drawing slow breaths, clawing internally for an ember of heat. He sat up, knees to his chest. Dearborn sat beside him on the bunk.

"Why are you doing this?" Baxter asked. "Why bother?"

"I'll tell you, but in the end it won't make any difference."

Baxter waited.

"You remember Balangiga?"

9

Baxter recovered from his injuries, although more than a week passed before he could breathe without significant pain. In the meantime, he had little to do but wait. Lind kept assuring him that a strike would develop, but there was no visible sign of one in town. After the days of mourning, the men went back to their scheduled work. Mr. Robertson was taking his time about responding to the report. No word had arrived from New York. With so little to occupy him, Baxter became jittery with idleness. He took to arranging the office files in more orderly rows, adding labels to some of the folders, and generally grousing about the uncertainty.

"You're in a hurry or something?" Lind asked.

"I just feel like we ought to be doing more."

"No use doing anything until we have to." Lind sat behind the desk, scribbling here and there in an open payroll ledger. "Right now the coal is coming out of the ground and going on the trains. We ought to hope that keeps up forever."

"I wish I had your patience."

"It's something you have to practice. Your job in the city would throw me off for sure. What is it you do again?"

Baxter prickled with insult, but Lind had barely looked his way in asking the question. Now Lind was waiting for an answer. He appeared genuinely to have forgotten. Was that plausible? "I began as one of Mr. Robertson's managing accountants, but our relationship has evolved over the years. He brings me in from time to time for special projects. I've worked in that capacity for him before."

"I remember now," Lind said. He straightened some papers. "Lunchtime, you know. Let's eat and talk."

Baxter followed him to the saloon, where a bar of polished oak stretched across the far end of the room. Over the shining brass rail, Lind ordered a pair of sandwiches and a pitcher of steam beer. Lind's guards, the only other patrons, had seated themselves along the wall. They were engrossed, hunched over their cards. Baxter and Lind found a table, and Lind said, "Yesterday Chamm sent a message back to union headquarters in Chicago. The men here want to walk, but they have to clear that first with the leadership. Otherwise a strike would be a wildcat, though not really because they've got no recognition right now. Anyway a strike won't have any teeth if the union don't support it."

"What was the response?"

"Don't know yet. Every once in a while the leaders turn them down, depending on how fat the strike funds are. The whole thing could just die out, but don't count on it."

"Why not?"

"Dunno. Just a hunch. Chamm's been ornery lately, before you got here, I mean. More sass than usual. The men might be itching for strife. But if headquarters backs them, it'll still be another few days until they're able to train-in supplies. My guess is you'll see an organizer or two show up before it's over."

"How in the world do you know all this?"

"Experience. Plus, the company reads whatever it wants to at the PO. It's our telegraph. We've got a right to know what goes over it. Whatever happens, we can respond in a lot of different ways."

Baxter took a long swallow from his beer. He continued to vacillate about Lind. At the moment his presence was a comfort. "It occurs to me that I haven't thanked you yet."

"For what?"

"Your knowledge and forthrightness. It's a rare man who's willing to be direct."

Lind raised his glass. They both drank. As they ate, however, an awkward silence opened between them. Baxter had spent his conversation on questions about the strike, and without work to discuss, other men became strange to him. He finished his meal and used a trip to the post office as an excuse to leave.

~

"I have *two* things for you today, Mr. Baxter," the clerk said. "Actually, one for you and one for Mr. Lind." He handed Baxter a telegram and a folded slip of paper.

Of the telegram, Baxter said, "When did you get this?"

"Came across the wire early this morning."

Baxter opened the message.

REPORT RECEIVED STOP MORE THAN SATISFACTORY STOP
STRIKE UNDERSTANDABLE GIVEN CIRCUMSTANCES STOP
WORK WITH LIND TOWARD RESOLUTION STOP
RECOMMENDATIONS UNDER ADVISEMENT STOP
P.D.R.

He loosened with relief. No shocks nor condemnations. He tucked Lind's message away and headed back to the office, to which Lind had returned.

"He's satisfied," Baxter said as he showed the message, "and the postmaster had this for you."

He handed over the second paper, which Lind skimmed.

"Strike's on," Lind said. "Union cleared the financing. You ready?"

"I'd better be."

Casually, Lind reached into his desk and tossed out a pistol. Baxter bobbled it but saved it from falling to the floor. The weapon felt alien and too heavy in his hand. "Are you sure I need this?"

"Take it just in case."

"I don't know how to use it."

"Don't worry. It ain't loaded."

"What should I do with it, then?"

"Just follow my lead."

They rounded up more guards and began a trudging march to the miners' housing on the hillside. Baxter knew perfectly well what was going to happen, yet he swallowed his reservations, trying to appear firm with the empty pistol in his belt.

The shacks were built of upright boards with narrow strips of rough lumber nailed over the cracks. Patches made from dry-goods crates, scrap boxes, corrugated iron, and old powder cans were also visible. In the breeze, the shacks creaked and swayed. The company had not spent a penny on them beyond the limits of barest necessity, and the only variation in their construction was the presence of row houses between the free-standing hovels, the former merely two or three rooms nailed together. Open privies and pit latrines were dug randomly about, stenching with a physical force.

At the first home, Lind whistled and pounded on the door. He took a few steps back and waited. A dark-haired man appeared. He was taller than Lind and heavily meated. Stone-faced, he dropped his hands into the pockets of his sunned-out overalls. "*Cosa vuoi?*"

"Out," Lind said.

The man stepped into the dirt, defiant. His hands, now fists, escaped his pockets but did not rise. Past him, Baxter could see inside to a woman and a child. They watched, distressed. "*E se non usciamo?*"

"We ain't waiting all day." Lind's interest wandered downhill, across the valley and the plain. "Move your ass."

"He doesn't understand," Baxter said.

"He knows exactly what we want."

"*Vaffa 'n culo. Noi restiamo qui.*"

"OUT!" Lind ordered. He drew the hammer back on his pistol, yet left it at his side.

The man looked at the gun, his lips moving soundlessly as if arguing with himself. "*Prendete le vostre cose. Dobbiamo andare.*"

"*Di nuovo?*" the woman replied from inside.

"*Ritorneremo un altro giorno ad ammazzarlo.*"

With the door ajar, Baxter could see her collecting a few belongings. He pulled Lind aside. "Can't we just evict the men?"

"Strikers can't stay in company housing."

"Wives and children aren't strikers."

"Close enough."

Baxter held his tongue after that. They moved from house to house, with Lind every once in a while dispensing a few shoves and loud commands, but the people endured the evictions with unexpected calm. Some of the workers did not even wait for a knock at the door, leaving of their own volition, figuring on inevitable eviction and, Baxter reasoned, wishing to avoid a confrontation. The lack of resistance was bewildering but certainly to be welcomed.

By late afternoon, in a long, snaking caravan, the strikers and their families had relocated to the plain. By evening, the exodus' accompaniment of rattling pots, clanking iron stoves, and the whining and crying of children had mostly died out.

Baxter went back to the office and rid himself of the pistol. He removed his hat and massaged his eyes. He felt bushed and unsettled about what he'd participated in, was disgusted a little by his own timidity. Still, the time to argue with the process had passed. He had not wanted to throw the situation off balance. Order was not to be cast aside lightly.

Despite the long day, Baxter wasn't hungry for dinner. He sat with Lorraine and Thomas as they ate. He touched nothing. He got a beer from the icebox. He could feel Lorraine's eyes on him.

"Quite a commotion on the plain today," she said.

"The union leadership approved the strike, so we had to evict everyone from the housing."

"Was that wise?"

"It's standard." He turned to Thomas, who was wearing his light wool sweater and fighting it where the prickly material met the bare skin of his neck. His head swiveled and twisted against the itching.

"Son, sit still, please. You're making me nervous."

"I hate this sweater."

"You'll get used to it. You have to wear something extra now that it's cool at night."

"Thank goodness we have a house to live in," Lorraine said.

Baxter threw on his overcoat and went outside. He could see his breath. Above, the stars made a sieve of the sky. He looked west to the horizon where the bluffs rose up as a single, enormous stair. The stars vanished in a jagged line behind the silhouette of the ridge. On the plain, fires in the strikers' camp winked and fluttered.

He drank from his beer and was overcome with the sensation of buoyancy that a small amount of alcohol can provide on an empty stomach. He closed his eyes and saw a man on a porch in Colorado with a town and canyons to the north and west, a makeshift city of unknown people on the dirt to the east, all in all a picture that should not contain him.

He set the bottle down. He'd expected the beer to relax him. Instead, after the lightness passed, he felt energized, agitated somehow. He knew he should do something productive if he was not going to sleep, but he did not feel at all like returning to his paperwork. He looked at the strikers' camp, at its glimmering fires, and then at the bluffs.

Reaching the shacks took him much longer than he expected. The beer gave him a distorted sense of the distance, and from the center of town, the shacks above did not appear any closer. Moreover, the lantern he'd found in the tool shed at the house provided a disappointing amount of light. The trails leading up to the hillside were difficult enough to navigate in the daytime, and now he had to keep to them in close to total darkness. However, he would have thought less of himself if he'd turned around and walked back, so he continued.

Even in the cool night, the latrines made themselves known halfway down the bluff wall, and he was in a full sweat as the first block of houses came clearly into view. He had flirted with a turned ankle along the way. Now he just wanted to get the inspection over with and go back home.

With the mines at rest and the men officially idle and relocated, Baxter was alone. He felt no hesitation about walking through the deserted homes. The shacks looked even more rickety and decrepit than he remembered. During the evictions, the people had perhaps distracted him from a close examination of the dwellings. He put his fingers into some of the holes in the walls. He peered through broken windows at remnant furniture, a bare bed frame here, a ragged cot there, interiors of scavenged lumber or corrugated tin or plain tar paper, floors of a single layer of planking, typically with dirt showing through in too many places.

He inspected for an hour until he felt he'd absorbed all he could. He walked through one last shack, the one at the head of the trail leading down to the town. Inside, he kicked aside empty food cans, cardboard boxes, and scraps of clothing, the same detritus he had seen in all the other vacancies.

"The Philippines?"

"Yes."

"You were there?"

"Yes."

Baxter remembered the headlines. Fifteen years past now. Comparisons to the Alamo, the Little Bighorn. He could not recall the last time he'd given a thought to the war with Spain. Mr. Robertson's friend Carnegie had cast his lot with Twain and the anti-imperialists. "The splendid little war."

"That's what Secretary Hay called it," Dearborn said. He talked of thatch huts on stilts. The church. The jungle. The swell of the gulf lifting and subsiding like a great blue lung. "When we landed, everyone was saying the war was over. I didn't expect anything but routine duty. And I didn't care much for why we were fighting in the first place. Cuba? The Philippines? Who could even find them on a map? I just wanted to finish my hitch."

A month of peace, then the surprise attack. Thirty-eight officers and men killed in fifteen minutes by axe and machete.

"In the end, only twenty-six of seventy-four were still breathing. Only four of us were unwounded. We never saw it coming. Eventually we fired back and escaped up the coast to Basey."

Baxter said, "I read about it."

"*The war went on and on,*" Dearborn said, lost in the retelling. *He spoke of his anger, revenges, water torture in which he jammed a bamboo tube into a prisoner's throat, filled him with putrid water to the point of death, and General Smith's orders to kill anyone over the age of ten. Two hundred thousand dead Filipinos.* "*We had no business there. Aguinaldo and his boys, it was their country. When I came stateside and McKinley called us heroes, I wanted to put a bullet in his head.*"

"*Somebody else took care of that for you.*"

Dearborn was quiet.

"*You didn't quit,*" Baxter said.

"*Soldiering was all I knew. You have to stay alive somehow. A man is nothing, sad to say. Once he's grown, he's finished. Life locks him up. He can't change. The only thing left is what he can do for another.*"

Baxter felt the texture of the wool blanket, the casual roughness of it on his shoulders. "*That was fifteen years ago.*"

Dearborn said, "*Fifteen years, fifteen seconds.*" *He sounded very far away. They sat together for a long time.* "*How are the blankets?*"

"*Thank you,*" Baxter said.

Dearborn stood and closed the cell door quietly. "*I'll see to it no one else bothers you.*"

10

Lind came to him with a purchase order. "We should send this tonight."

Baxter balked as he read the list. "Barbed wire? Chain-link fencing?"

"We need to fortify the property."

"But we have these materials already. Do we need this much more?"

"Maybe not, but you can't be too careful about reinforcement."

"And this here?" Baxter said, jabbing the paper. "Searchlights for the ridges? Let's not lose our heads."

"We've been meaning to install lights for a good while. You can cable the Denver office if you don't believe me. I put in for them a long time ago, but they never arrived. A clerk on their end must have lost the order."

"And you didn't follow up on it?"

"Sure I did. But there's only so much time in a day. I badgered them once or twice before I had to go back to running your mine."

"I still don't see the purpose."

"We'll be able to light up that squatter's camp so bright they'll think it's noon at midnight. The more we can see what's going on, the better. Plus, when the strike is over, all that extra light will help out the night shifts."

With reluctance, Baxter signed the order, convincing himself it was only prudent to take precautionary measures before commencing negotiations. Days later, when the goods arrived from Denver, he found himself helping to transport them from the supply train to the base of the bluffs. From there, everything light enough to carry was lugged by hand to the higher driftmouths. Gear too heavy for men was towed and dragged up the switchbacks on mule-drawn carts. The crates of parts for the searchlights were the worst of the lot. Like caskets for a race of giants, the crates were too long and wide to fit in any of the carts, so the men had to work in teams of four to carry the ponderous boxes to the top. By the time Baxter made his third trip to the ridge, he felt akin to the ancient pyramid builders.

When Lind whistled a half hour break, Baxter sat panting near the edge of the bluff. The high vantage revealed the coke ovens, the tipple and the water tank to the east, the secondary railroad tracks arcing to the southeast and northwest. Beyond the town, the burgeoning camp of strikers lay below on the plain. He could also see the company shacks. Men and women continued to scuttle up to them, toting off the stray items they hadn't been able to carry during the initial eviction. Shelters and precarious small tents of sticks and spare clothing had sprung up in the camp. Stove chimneys poked a short way into the sky and exhaled rusty smoke. As his eyes traced the lone rail line sweeping north out of the valley, the notion of quarantine rose to his mind. The track might be the only permitted connection to a town raging with plague. In the opposite direction, the canyons—brown, labyrinthine, immense—folded over themselves to the horizon.

He recovered his wind and drank gratefully from a canteen. Nearby, Lind unrolled blueprints on a makeshift table of two sawhorses and a large plank of wood. With rocks, Baxter weighed down the curled edges of the paper. He admired the detailed layout of the valley, from the location of the housing and the commercial structures to all the company's shafts, the whole of the property depicted in soundless order.

Lind's men drifted in from the other ridges, crawling back from the jagged edges of the mesa and eating a hurried lunch around the blueprints. Lind circled the driftmouths in the order he wanted them fortified, roughly from the bottom up, since the lower shafts were more easily accessed from town level. By six o'clock, most of the searchlights had been assembled, a crate of spare parts sitting beside each, and the extra barbed wire had been apportioned and distributed to the shafts. At dusk, on the way down the bluff, Lind pulled a flask from his vest. "Long day," he said. "Take a snort."

Baxter did. The whiskey burned into him and felt good. In the distance, a dust trail rose into the air from beyond where the northern track disappeared over the horizon. "Train's coming in," Baxter said. "I thought all of our shipments arrived already."

"They did."

"So, who's that?"

"The union."

~

Through the following days, Baxter watched in wonderment as a small city rose from the plain. Stakes were driven into the ground to define walkways running parallel to the line of town buildings, and at the opposite end of each walkway a deep hole was dug for a latrine. From the supply trains came lumber, bolls of canvas, and tents of all types—umbrella tents of dark brown canvas, the stunted triangular tubes of pup tents, large surplus military troop tents spacious enough for three families apiece. Food arrived, too. Sacks of potatoes and oats, sacks of flour and ground corn, cases of canned goods.

Something of a competition developed between the company and the miners with respect to mutual bracings, the company with installations of padlocked wire enclosures around each driftmouth, the strikers with the continual influx of supplies from the union. Apart from the empty union cars, the only other trains moving out of the valley were those drawing down coal from the tipple.

Lind advocated for intrusive searches of each union shipment, but Baxter vetoed him, allowing the camp to be constructed unmolested. In his view, any climate conducive to negotiation would have to begin with the physical safety of the strikers.

"We can do whatever we want to on company property," Lind said. "Why give them space to relax?"

"The plain is federal land," Baxter said. "The rail beds are privately held, but not by the company."

"Can't we buy them?"

"Buying railroads isn't like buying bread. Mr. Robertson has been trying for years to gain a monopoly of the shipping and railroad companies. I've even seen some of the acquisition contracts. The men who own those industries don't want to sell. They may not be as powerful as Mr. Robertson, but they've got enough capital to make nuisances of themselves. How do you think they would react to continuous search and seizure of shipments on their cars?"

"It worked in '94."

"The Pullman strike? Not comparable. This isn't something we can solve by attaching mail cars to the trains."

"Why not?"

"When we did it then—that's to say, when Mr. Robertson suggested it—President Cleveland had to endorse it and then pass orders to the attorney general. Only then could the union be enjoined for interference with the mails."

"It worked," Lind said again.

"Yes, but only because it was interference on the *workers'* part. If *we* stop those trains, it's interference on the company's part."

"You were just a kid back then."

"That's right, but I'm a grown man now, and I've studied history. I can tell you that President Wilson is no President Cleveland, not with Roosevelt and Debs on his tail. The Progressives already won the income tax and the direct election of senators. And last year the Democrats swept all three branches. Do you really want *that* gang looking into what's happening here? I certainly don't, but mucking around with those trains will guarantee scrutiny."

"I don't see it that way."

"I know, but you're wrong. We all have our areas of expertise, and corporate acquisitions is not one of yours." Baxter insisted that no searches be authorized unless there was good reason to believe contraband was being imported.

Lind swallowed hard and agreed.

The rock. Its roughness and heft. He could still feel the pull on his palm. He thought, And if Lind had been conscious, watchful? A pair of open eyes might have proved an unbreachable barrier. No. Embrace the truth. Dispel the illusion. Look even now how blind optimism hangs on. Tenacious, vicious parasite. A wounded and cornered rat. After all that's passed, a wakeful gaze would have stopped you? Another lie. Spare yourself. The rock would have fallen just the same, just as repeatedly. Had Lind brought his hands to his face for a shield, you would have smashed all the harder. But Lind had not done that. He'd been only an unconscious man, a vessel of burns and injuries. And for you, afterward, joy and a warmth deeper still.

Baxter opened and closed his hand. The jagged weight, a residence in his skin. He had not struck with the first rock on which his hand lighted. He remembered very clearly, turning to the side and choosing from among many within reach. Some were too large and heavy, some too awkwardly shaped. The one he chose required his stump, too, for control. When he felt the rock's weight, he knew it would suffice. Lind, meanwhile, waited, insensate.

Consequences dissipated like moisture in the high desert heat. Consider the tunnels. What was one more body, more or less? No use dodging now.

Lind. Helpless.

He felt sick. A man might be nothing. To kill a man might therefore be nothing. But to kill and feel what he felt while killing? Something quite different. He turned the notion over several times, inspecting it from all sides, wishing to have felt nothing or merely satisfaction. What he'd felt instead was worse beyond imagining.

Now the soldiers. Judgment passed to them.

So much ruin. He so desperately wanted to know where exactly the process had begun. He could say of himself that he had done only what another man in his place would have done. He could say this easily, for anything can be said easily. Words alone make nothing true.

The choice, perhaps relinquished when he lied to enter the mine. That was a violation. Perhaps farther back when he joined the company, knowing the way of companies. He'd read enough to know. The difference, then, between knowing with the mind and knowing with the flesh. Perhaps no difference, no boundary to traverse. Perhaps he had been pushed. Perhaps Lind had pushed him.

Perhaps, perhaps. Peace, a long way off. Maybe as it should be, he thought. I might no longer know its face.

11

The strikers fashioned a baseball diamond on the plain, which Baxter regarded as a good sign. People who felt secure enough to play baseball should be open to a proposal for talks. He waited for a game to begin before making an approach. Along the base lines, the miners' wives and families sat on the ground. When a line-drive zipped into the outfield, cheers went up on both sides as the spectators rose to their feet, but the left fielder nabbed the ball and made the out, and the crowd deflated as the fielders jogged in for offense.

No time like the present, Baxter thought. He stepped onto the field. "Excuse me, folks. I need to speak with someone." A few heads turned toward him and quieted, triggering a cascade of silence through the crowd. "Excuse me," he said again. "I'm sorry to interrupt your game, but I have to talk to you. Do you have a representative? Is Mr. Chamm here?"

Baxter looked around. He recognized no one, and no one said anything. His stomach began to churn. He walked to the batter, whose bat was slung across his shoulders, hands dangling.

"You, sir," Baxter said. "Don't you want to go back to work?"

"*Ti stacco la testa con questo se fai un altro passo.*" He gripped the bat with both hands and brandished it, moving forward. "*Vaffa 'n culo,*" he said. "*Pezzo di merda.*"

Baxter backed up precipitously. "Wait, wait, you don't understand."

"Course he don't," Chamm said, emerging from the crowd. He waved off the batter and the man withdrew, but from the sidelines someone else let loose at Chamm, again in a foreign language. Chamm wheeled and replied in kind before turning to Baxter. "Can't you leave us alone for just a few hours? Time ago I heard a working-man was entitled to a little rest. I'm gettin' tired of pullin' your nuts out of the fire."

Baxter marveled at Chamm's fluency. "Was that Greek?"

"The second time. First was Italian."

"How many languages do you speak?"

"Bits and pieces of a bushel. I get by. Spend as much time around these folks as me, you'd pick up a few words, too."

"It's extraordinary."

"What's the matter, Baxter? Never seen a hillbilly with a talent before?"

Baxter cleared his throat. "You need to nominate a representative."

"We know."

"That's the usual procedure."

"Don't shit the nest. The union's already picked him. He just ain't in town yet."

"Have him come and see me when he arrives."

"Sure thing. That all?"

"Yes."

"Can we go back to our game now?"

"Of course, of course." Uncertain of how to conclude, Baxter offered his hand, and Chamm shook it with a bemused, almost pitying smile.

Baxter walked back to the sidelines. He could feel the stares pushing him away. A snigger ran through the crowd as the game recommenced, and as he crossed through the line of buildings to Main Street, he could not help feeling vaguely humiliated even though he'd accomplished what he'd set out to do.

Nor did dinner relieve his sense of failure. Hours afterward, he was still fixated on the game. He went into the kitchen at the rattle of the teakettle. Lorraine struck many matches before the burner lit successfully. He placed a hand on the small of her back and kissed her on the neck. She lifted the lid of the tea jar. "Do you want some?"

"No, thank you." He walked to the refrigerator, took out a beer, and sat down. "I started negotiations today. I think I did, anyway."

"What does that mean?"

"I told them to designate a representative."

"And?"

"They already have one."

"What's he like?"

"I don't know. I haven't met him yet. He'll be here soon."

Lorraine poured water over her tea leaves. "Sounds like everything is on track."

"You'd think so, wouldn't you?"

She sat down next to him. "Mr. Lind must have something to say about all this."

"Oh, he's got plenty to say." Baxter thought of the crowd at the game. "They were playing baseball today. You should have seen them. They looked so ragged." He sipped from his beer. "A tent city," he said. "It's appalling that things have come to this."

Lorraine did not reply. She stirred her tea for an inordinately long time, clinking the spoon on the side of the cup.

"Tell me," he said.

"It's not important."

"I want to know what's on your mind."

She set the spoon down on the saucer. "No one forced them to strike."

"Lorraine, those people have nothing. Without work, they haven't been earning scrip, which means the commissary has been closed to them. I don't even know if they had food before their supplies arrived."

"They should have anticipated that before striking, don't you think?"

Baxter drummed his fingers on his beer bottle.

"I'm not saying they should have been evicted, but they did have jobs and housing. I wouldn't call that nothing. Not everyone can be wealthy, you know. And I'll bet there are a lot of wives in those tents saying exactly the same thing to their husbands right now."

"The company should just cast them off?"

"Of course not."

"Then what do you suggest?"

"I suggest you tuck in your son. He's waiting upstairs." She yawned and kissed him good night. Baxter trailed her up the stairs.

~

Thomas' room was sparsely furnished, making it appear more capacious than it was in reality. Abutting his bed were the small dresser and the stack of picture books he'd brought along from New York.

Baxter sat down on the edge of the bed. He pushed the boy's hair from his forehead and laid on an extra quilt against the cold. Thomas squirmed around, battling the covers in an attempt to situate himself comfortably. Only after he stilled was Baxter allowed back into his universe.

"All settled?"

Thomas nodded.

"There was a baseball game today," Baxter said.

"Really?"

"The entire camp was playing, but it was all adults."

"I wish there were more kids here. I wish I didn't have to stay near the house all day."

"I know," Baxter said. "You'll just have to tolerate it for now. It wouldn't be safe for you in town. Don't worry. We'll be back in New York soon enough."

"When?"

"When the strike is over. When the people go back to work."

"A man said they should freeze to death."

"What man?"

"One of the guards."

Baxter paused for a moment over how to counter his son, trying to remind himself of what it was like to be a child, the world an ongoing spectacle scrubbed of history and context. "When did you hear that?"

"When I walked with Mom for groceries. I heard him say it in town."

"She didn't mention it."

Thomas rolled away from him. "I wish we were in New York now."

Baxter did not want to pursue the matter. It was time for the boy to sleep. Discussion could wait. "Look at me, please."

Thomas rolled back.

"That man should have kept his opinion to himself."

"Why?"

"You tell me."

"What he said wasn't very nice."

"That's right. And what else?"

"No one should have to freeze to death."

"Good."

"But they did something bad, right?"

"Not exactly."

"What did they do?"

"It's not important. The point is, don't believe everything people say."

"Why not?"

So much for avoiding a discussion. "Because people lie. Haven't you ever told a lie?"

Thomas watched his father warily.

"Don't worry. I'm not going to punish you."

"Yes," Thomas said. "But I try not to. I feel bad when I do."

"As you should."

"But sometimes I feel bad about telling the truth."

"Like when?"

"One time, we got a new kid in class whose arm was messed up. It looked like what dolphins have."

"A flipper."

"The teacher told us just to ignore it because it wasn't his fault, and there wasn't anything he could do about it."

"That was good advice."

"But that was lying, wasn't it, pretending not to see his arm?"

"In a sense, yes."

"But shouldn't we always tell the truth?"

"Up to a point. It's complicated. A lot of things have to be taken on a case-by-case basis."

Thomas pulled the covers to his chin and relaxed into the pillow. Baxter wasn't sure if he was mulling things over, or if he'd switched completely to thinking about something else. In any case, he asked no more questions. Baxter turned off the light and went across the hall.

"I think we're raising a lawyer," he said as he climbed into bed.

Lorraine looked up from her book. "What?"

"Nothing."

When Hawkins' body fell, gave up its blood to the snow, Lind spat on it with a look, his declaration of what weakness deserves. The last moment, then, of a peace that might have held, maybe not forever, but for a while longer, long enough to extricate himself. To do his job and exit.

"You were doing it all the while," Hawkins would have said, "doing it and refusing to accept what it was, what you were."

The strikers surged forward and were pounded back, falling with shouts and dull thuds before another span of injured stasis. In that moment, Lind offered the pistol. I declined it, Baxter thought, which did no good whatsoever. What if I'd taken it? I might have learned otherwise of weakness. Transfixed. The awful red against the white snow. He tore his eyes away. Action, impossible at the time. Sight sufficed. Afterward, no longer numbers on paper. Real men and real lives and real blood and real earth that drank it. He watched and thought that some force within things would surely bring all to a halt, for life requires an arbiter, calls one forth when the situation demands. Well, no. The squall passed for the night. The scabs moved on. The strikers picked themselves up. The corpse was collected and toted away. Death glanced about with detachment and advanced another step. Had the ground lacked snow, Hawkins' blood would have looked black on it, rainwater on summer dust. Less shocking, no less consequential. Baxter felt nauseated and overcome. The earth will never be saturated.

Men contain nowhere near the blood to saturate it, and still they may never stop.

Barbarity, love, cruelty, justice, hate. Empty, pointless, useless words. All red and warm. Their power to heal, overstated. He felt pain for certain, and endured the nights as he paced. Food from Dearborn on the first. No talk. Then the second. Push it under, he thought. Now the third. The last. Before, days and nights on the porch, waiting. Alone. And before that, the tunnels.

He wished for the tunnels again, though not for the conflict and violence. He was glad to be through. But Dearborn's story had triggered a longing. The tunnels, the stories. He wished he still had them. Deranged, this nostalgia. Yet only the stories had driven Lorraine and Thomas from his mind.

This is history. How it works. Supine and ignored for so long, it mimics death, even sends up a stench. Then one of its hands shoots out and relieves you of your heart. Garris' stories kept him sane. The other men's stories kept him sane. Sanity through diversion. Someone take my mind away until it no longer has to function. He thought of the others again, of what he'd done for them and if he'd really done it for them. He thought of what he'd done and asked if it could be called sane.

12

"Did we not fight the Civil War to end slavery?" boomed the man at the podium. "Of course we did!"

Baxter was walking home from the commissary, a bag of groceries heavy in his arms, when he saw the assembly. The strikers and their families had amassed before a wooden platform. He moved close enough to hear, but did not enter the crowd. The entire encampment had turned out. The speaker appeared to be of Baxter's age but with a boxer's build and thinning brown hair that stood from his head.

"But wage slavery is kin to chattel slavery! By what lunatic logic do we allow ourselves to be rented out like second-hand mules? What kind of bizarre prank is this that we're playing on ourselves?"

Wonderful, Baxter thought. A Socialist in full plumage. Lind will be thrilled.

Chamm came abreast of him, smiling and thumbing at the speaker. "Meet the rep."

"Debs wasn't available?"

"This guy'll do."

"His name, please?"

"Hawkins. Max Hawkins."

"Property should not be owned and controlled by the few. It should be distributed equally, administered democratically for the benefit of all. Power should not rest in the hands of the few. It should be distributed equally, wielded democratically for the benefit of all. These are simple ideas, my friends. A child could understand them."

The men before Hawkins grumbled, heads nodding in assent.

Baxter nudged Chamm. "You're not buying any of this, are you?"

"Truth hurt, don't it, boss?"

"You're wasting your skills. You should be translating."

"Speechin's like a good rain, Baxter. Every drop don't need to hit you to clean you off a little. Anyhow, the union prints up translations ahead of time. Whatever language you want. Look." He pointed at the pamphlets which were all about in hands and protruding from pockets. "We give 'em a read, hash 'em out a little beforetime. Hawkins comes around for the show after that. It's more fun that way."

"What of those stinking and puerile sycophants called Democrats and Republicans? Their throats are hoarse. Freedom, they preach. Prosperity, they cry. And you live in the dirt, in a tent if you're lucky. You work at the point of a gun. You sweat and die in those bluffs over there, and the products of your labor are spirited away to the lair of some New York crone who hoards them up like a dragon. This is outrageous, citizens! That coal is a public resource! One man shouldn't have the right to own and control it! Has the merest spark of charity ever passed through Robertson's black heart? Has he ever tended to anything other than his riches? Every cent of his boodle drips with the enslaved blood of ordinary men and women, and his only thought is, How can I get more?"

The grumbles rose again, this time accompanied by scattered applause. Someone passed Hawkins a cup of water from which he refreshed himself. "But do not think, brothers and sisters, that in amassing his vast fortune Paul David Robertson has subverted the spirit of this country. Do not think that for a single moment. His lapdogs in Washington know exactly what he is doing. They're not being hoodwinked. In fact, they support him! And who among you will be surprised by that? Who will be surprised by their greed and corruption? This government thrives on greed and corruption! Greed and corruption were from the first days its animating spirit! Brothers and sisters, the Constitution was not designed to enhance your welfare, but rather to destroy it! Have you not read the words of James Madison, the great author of our bedrock document, the same James Madison who said that the purpose of government is to protect the minority of the opulent against the majority? He said that at the Constitutional Convention, no less! Did not John Jay, our first chief justice, say that the men who own the country ought to govern it? Of course he did, brothers and sisters, of course he did."

Baxter wondered how many hours Hawkins had spent in the library, selecting his barbs. With his dark suit gone dusty and his thick hands like clubs, from a distance he could have been mistaken for T.R., although he lacked Roosevelt's boiler of a torso. Still, as he pounded the air, the similarity of gestures was striking.

"And how wonderfully it all worked out for them, for who else governs the country other than its owners? What else has government done than protect the rich from the poor? It's been one hundred and thirty-seven years since that gaggle of slaveholders, embezzlers, and stock-jobbers established their continental enterprise of exploitation and pillage, and who runs it now? The same contemptible ruling class that ran it then!"

Hawkins wiped his brow to more applause and a peppering of huzzahs. "But do not despair, citizens. We are not here to make a demon of government. Government is only an instrument, a shadow of the powers that control the society. And from time to time even within government there have been great men sympathetic to our ideas. Jefferson, for one, who dreamed and wrote of freedom, only to see his vision perverted by capital. Thomas Paine, who never forgot the importance of brotherhood and solidarity. Lincoln, too, who thought that corporations were a greater threat to the Union than the secession of the South. Think about *that* for a moment. The most Lincoln could do was keep America alive and preside over the end of slavery. That was quite a lot, to be sure, but it wasn't enough. He couldn't rescue America from the grip of its ruling class. He wept as his country writhed, but he couldn't rescue it."

"Consider, then, Jefferson, Paine, and Lincoln. Isolated individuals, citizens. Alone, there was a limit to what they could accomplish. But you are not alone, brother. Sister, you are not alone. The people are here with you today as you are with them, the people in whose name America was founded and whose well-being its ruling class has always subverted—out of fear, you understand, out of fear of our collective power. And they are wise to do it, too, because when someday very soon the people control America, its government will be *our* shadow, *our* tool, and with it we will *smash* privilege. We will *destroy* plutocracy."

Baxter looked at Chamm, who was positively gleeful. Chamm clapped him on the back. "Don't worry, boss man, he's almost through." Despite himself, Baxter let out a guffaw.

"Friends, we have no choice but to embrace this struggle. If we fail to act, if we shirk the duty history has bequeathed to us, we can foresee the result. We know exactly what the Paul David Robertsons of the world have in store for us if we lie down to be flogged: poverty, disease, vice, starvation, fear, and madness, and death. You *know* that will be our reward, citizens, for it's the time-honored recompense of slaves. And never, never will it include the one thing we desire most. JUSTICE, brothers and sisters! JUSTICE! Power does not want to give us that, but, by God, WE WILL HAVE IT!"

The applause struck in a hammer of sound as Hawkins stepped away from the podium. He wiped his brow again, bowing and waving as the assembly boiled with enthusiasm, throwing hats into the air and spilling forward. The men lifted Hawkins to their shoulders.

Baxter's ears rang with the noise, and he felt no animosity. He'd seen enough of the difficulties in these people's lives to excuse a little venting. At least now the negotiations could start. "You think they followed all that?" he shouted to Chamm.

"They know he's punching for us. Don't need much more than that."

"Tell Mr. Hawkins to come see me in the office when the festivities are over."

Baxter went on his way, and soon heard the thump of hooves on Main Street, which was ordinary enough, but as the sound grew, he stopped. The town didn't host enough horses to produce what he was hearing. Through the string of buildings, streams of mounted men poured. Baxter dove aside too late. A billy club caught him square across the chest. The bag of groceries absorbed most of the blow. A horse's bulk passed over him, and the hair of its tail lashed his face. The riders clubbed anything that moved in the crowd, now panicked and screaming.

Incensed, Baxter picked himself up and ran into the fray. "Stop! Stop right now!" His throat cinched with anger and betrayal. Pinkertons. They had to be. He couldn't believe Lind had called them in without his consent or even advice. Baxter had seen no sign of their arrival the day before, so Lind must have trained them in at night and camped them beyond the tipple for secrecy. Nowhere else on the plain provided cover. Baxter bellowed, "I absolutely demand that you stop this right now!"

One of the riders buckled his knees with a club. "The next one splits your head," the rider said, careening on to another target.

The crowd thinned as some of the people escaped back into the camp. Then the horses swept into a circle, trapping Baxter and others inside a cordon. Paradoxically, confinement calmed the situation by inspiring a moment of frightened passivity.

"Stay firm, folks," Hawkins said from somewhere within the circle. "No way out right now. Be patient."

"Listen to your friend," a rider said to the crowd.

"What's the story here?" Hawkins asked him.

"Gotta take you away. You're inciting a riot."

"Ahh. What's your name, friend?"

"Never mind that."

"I didn't see anything like a riot here, leastways not until you and your boys showed up. We were just having a nice, pleasant meeting. Just a bunch of friends discussing the circumstances of their lives, you see? You might find you've got a lot in common with them."

"We can't have you rabble-rousing."

Hawkins turned to his audience. "Are you rabble? Are you roused?"

"Enough of this," another rider said. He drew the horses into a tighter circle.

"Hang on, hang on," Hawkins said, again with pleasantness. "Am I to assume that you're taking us to jail?"

"Damn right."

"Fair enough, but you've trapped women and children here. Shouldn't you let them out first?"

The mounted men looked at each other. One of them said, "We can't fit *all* of them in the cell."

Another agreed, saying, "We'll open up so the women and children can go home. Any men try to go, we shoot 'em down."

"Excellent. Agreed. *Solo donne e bambini,*" Hawkins said. "*Tylko kobiety i dzieci.*"

"What did you tell them?" a rider demanded. "What did you say?"

"Only what we agreed on: women and children. My pronunciation is awful. The words come out like half chewed food, but folks usually understand. Unfortunately, in our business we need to know those words in a lot of languages, right?"

The rider ignored him, but one of the horses peeled away from the circle. The wives and children trickled out, and then the cordon closed again.

Baxter moved to the perimeter of the group until he was against one of the horses. "You don't understand," he said to the rider. "I'm an official here."

"Sure."

"My name is Baxter. Ask Lind who I am."

"Shut your trap."

~

The men crammed into the cell, the first of them tripping and scrambling out from under the soles of those following. Baxter was shoved forward. He caught himself against the rear wall as he stumbled. He tried to flatten himself into inconspicuousness as the last of the miners tumbled in with Hawkins. The door swung shut with a clank. Baxter's eyes lit about for Chamm, but he was not present.

The jailers withdrew to the booking room. A huge dark-haired striker stared fiercely after them, and when they were gone, he turned toward the interior of the cell, muttering and spitting with frustration. His gaze fell upon Baxter and his face lit with rage. He pushed forward, fist raised.

Baxter tried to retreat, but he'd forgotten how close he was to the wall. Trapped, he closed his eyes and braced himself.

The blow never arrived.

After a few moments, Baxter opened his eyes, and the others burst out laughing at him. He flushed with embarrassment. Hawkins had stopped the assault. His hand was still clamped around the dark-haired man's wrist.

Baxter could do nothing until the ridicule died out, so he simply tried to stiffen his posture enough to preserve some dignity. "Wipe that smirk off your face," he said to Hawkins.

"Now, now. Is that any way to address a man who just saved you a beating?"

"I can take a punch just fine, thank you. I don't need you to protect me."

"I'll remember that." He offered his hand. "Max Hawkins."

Baxter declined the greeting.

"Please, sir," Hawkins prodded. "Good manners never harmed anyone."

Reluctantly, Baxter reciprocated. "Harlan Baxter."

Hawkins broke into a grin. "I thought so. It's wonderful to finally meet you. Mr. Chamm told me about you, but he hadn't a chance to point you out yet."

"I figured he would be in here with us."

"He must have escaped before the thugs closed ranks. He thinks quite charitably of you."

"Sure he does."

"It's true."

"How so?"

"Not every corporate stooge can survive a twelve-hour shift in a Colorado mine."

"What happened to your respect for manners?"

"Indeed," Hawkins said. "I apologize. Nonetheless, the point holds."

"That shift almost killed me."

"But you persevered, and that says something."

"The negotiations have to start immediately."

"Don't be impatient. We'll get around to them. In any case, I doubt you'll be here with us long enough to discuss anything of substance."

Baxter took off his tie, sweat prickling him as the cell simmered with the collective wait. The men groused in soft sullenness, and the motionless air filled with their rank and humid breath.

Hawkins inhaled deeply, appearing to relax. "So much for the First Amendment."

"What?"

"Come on, Baxter. You've heard of it. Freedom of speech. The right to assemble. The right to petition for the redress of grievances. Fat lot of good they do us, eh? Use them to stand up for ourselves and look what happens."

"As if you haven't been in this position before."

"More times than I can count." Hawkins sat down as men moved aside for him. "I'm a connoisseur of our country's jails." He slapped the floor with his hand. "This one is solid enough. Standard. Well-built."

"If you enjoy it so much, I can see to it that you stay here for a long time."

"When they locked Debs and his comrades away after the Pullman strike, the Cook County jail was filthy with cobwebs and piss. The rats were so big that the sheriff's fox terrier ran away from them in fear. The prisoners were stripped to waist and locked in the dark for twenty hours a day. They spent their time scratching at rat bites until blood ran down their chests. But in the end, all the men went home satisfied. Do you know why? Because in an unjust world, a prison cell is the only home of a righteous man."

"Oh, for chrissakes."

"My point is, don't expect us to be deterred by a little crowding. The people are made of sterner stuff than that."

"Fancy yourself a Bull Moose, do you?"

"I should think not. We tried to denude that wolf-in-sheep's-clothing in the last election. What kind of reformer accepts the existence of corporate feudal lords? Roosevelt is a fraud and a latent Caesar to boot. This is the first time I've shared a cell with a member of the landed gentry, however."

"I hope you're not referring to me."

"I'll bet you even went to Harvard."

"Sorry, no."

"Well, well, then! You really are one of the rabble! Maybe you do belong in here with the rest of us."

"Who are you kidding? That was no street urchin's speech you gave out there."

"It's true. I graduated from Princeton. Class of '94."

"Quite a contradiction, wouldn't you say?"

"Not necessarily. The upper classes can sympathize with the lower classes."

"I expect you to remember that."

A booking clerk walked through the outer door.

"You don't seem all that sympathetic," Hawkins said. "If you were, you would know already."

"I'm finished talking to you."

The clerk clanged a metal pipe against the bars. "Listen up! Nobody but Baxter moves to the door. There are plenty of guards outside so don't even try."

"I told you your liberation would soon be at hand," Hawkins said.

"Excuse me," Baxter said as he pushed forward. The clerk unlocked the door, and Baxter walked out as it closed again with a heavy iron clang. "Exactly what should I know?"

"You're on the wrong side."

~

As Baxter stomped off toward the office, successive waves of anger broke over him, first at Lind for having taken such a provocative step without clearance, and then just as strongly at Hawkins. On the wrong side? He was on the side of sense! Of sanity! The carelessness of all involved was shocking. One doesn't just stride into the middle of a delicate situation and begin throwing verbal bombs. What did Hawkins expect would happen, even if no men with clubs and guns were about? And what about Lind, since *he'd* been the instigator? From within the crowd, Baxter hadn't felt any stirrings of violence. The people were a little raucous, but they were only listening until Lind's men showed up. Confronting Lind at the office, Baxter commanded, "Explain where those men came from," and Lind's nonplussed expression only made him angrier.

"I wired a few friends I know from the old days. Don't worry. They won't strain the budget too badly."

"The budget?" Baxter said, stupefied. "I'm talking about the attack! I wound up in jail!"

"Sorry about that. The men don't know everybody in town yet."

"I was wearing a shirt and tie!"

"You were at a rally. They must have figured you for an agitator."

"You disobeyed my direct orders."

Lind's eyes drew out to slits. "Follow me," he said, walking outside where a wagon was hitched to two horses pawing at the dirt. Lind hoisted himself into the wagon and took the reins. Hesitantly, Baxter climbed aboard, and Lind whipped the horses into motion. The wagon jounced away and, spitting to empty his mouth of the dust kicked up by the horses, Baxter locked his hands to the side panels. The wagon cleared the north end of Main Street and continued toward the depot where a few boxcars had been shunted from the main track and were surrounded by guards.

Lind hauled back on the reins and the horses squealed in pain, skidding to a stop. Lind jumped down, pulling Baxter with him. He waved off the guards and approached one of the boxcars.

"Union supply train came in this morning from Denver," Lind said. "We had a tip something was up."

He climbed through the sliding door. Baxter trailed him, wiping dirt from his eyes and blinking to regain his sight as the glare of the sun gave way to the darkness of the car's interior. The car was half filled with long wooden crates variously labeled as foodstuffs. Lind walked to a crate and opened it. Inside, blankets were folded neatly and stacked to the rim.

"So?" Baxter said.

Lind pushed the blankets aside, and an array of weapons, maybe two dozen rifles, gleamed blackly from within.

"Sweet Jesus," Baxter said.

"And these are just the ones we know about."

Stop, stop, stop. Done with, over and done with. Control and restraint. Hold together until morning. Focus on what's palpable. Heat from the pacing, enough to rest. He sat down on the floor with the tail of the blanket beneath him for insulation, his body wrapped like a Sioux's.

So wonderful on that day to watch Garris lean on the first detonator, toss the plain into the sky. No denying the happiness. He should have felt shame, but shame had been immeasurably distant from his heart. The explosions were the most magnificent sight in all creation. His thoughts fell on how many of Lind's men died in the first blast. The answer came easily: Not enough.

The tracks to Denver, destroyed, yet Dearborn's men, fully equipped, arrived. The old man had readied them long in advance. If he'd waited for word from Lind's last men, weeks would have elapsed before Dearborn appeared. Prepared as always, Baxter thought. Set up the last maneuver and then wait. Keep it from the press. Let events unfold on their own. Lind's crew had not been sufficient for victory. No matter. Always more force. Always more resources. Both can be applied at will. Why do anything rash?

Dearborn, suspicious, may have sent men into the canyons. No matter on that, too. All that could be done for them had been done. I'm doing it now, he thought. This is my job now, Hawkins. I've given them a reprieve. Something to work with.

Baxter slumped. He kept his arm immobile in his lap. The wad of cloth held intact. From the driftmouth the men had watched the flight of Lind's last men. Garris, successful, turned his face toward Baxter, lifted a skeptical eyebrow devoid of celebration.

Yes. No real joy here because this keeps going forever. No need to medicate with sentiment. He wished he'd asked Garris how long it takes for endurance to become a countenance. Months since I've seen my own face. What sick dirt it must be tracked with now. Bearded and thin. Where once lived flesh, the skull protrudes. My legs are straw. The bones of my feet are the veins of dried-out leaves. My skin creeps with lice and revulsion. Inside, all is sand and spent fire.

He thought of Garris and those with him in the canyons.

Go, he thought.

Go.

13

Buildings dominated his childhood, his earliest memory a mountainous cube of stone and brick with a long shard jutting from the top. His father was beside him, both of them looking skyward. The tower fell endlessly as the clouds swam behind it, and Baxter was transfixed, confused by the one huge circle pasted on an assembly of squares. He was four years old, pointing up.

"It's a clock," his father said. "The long tower is called a steeple. Architecture is America's greatest talent, Harlan." Later he would learn the name: the Tribune Building, on Nassau and Spruce Street.

In the Civil War, Cyrus Baxter served under Roebling as an engineer, proofing the plans for the bridge over the Rappahannock, twelve hundred feet long upon its completion. He'd helped with a suspension across the Shenandoah at Harper's Ferry. Roebling liked to ride the hot air balloon on its morning ascent to surveil the enemy. "He saw General Lee from that balloon, heading towards Gettysburg. And at Little Round Top, Roebling placed the first cannon and held off the rebels. He might have saved the union."

Cyrus had stories, too, about the Brooklyn Bridge, unceasing stories. Roebling cudgeled the legislature into authorizing it, and Cyrus' old association with him was sufficient to land a job on the project. Cyrus always preluded with winters. '66 when ice choked the East River for days at a time. Ferries were cancelled or stranded in floes. Business was delayed in Manhattan. Intolerable. The bridge would fix everything. Then fire nearly consumed the Brooklyn caisson, and men were dropping dead from digging in the mud all day. "And still the towers grew. A month or so after the Centennial they strung a single rope between the Brooklyn and New York towers. Some lunatic named Farrington volunteered to make the first trip across the river on a pulley and a swing. I read the announcement to your mother, God rest her soul, and she said, 'We can't miss that,' so we put you in a basket and took you with us on the ferry."

They watched with field glasses from mid-river as Farrington, dapper in his linen suit and bowler, waved from atop the Brooklyn tower, draped like its Manhattan twin with a huge American flag. He plopped into his two-foot wide boatswain chair and inched across the river.

"It was insanity," his father said, beaming with the recounting. "Pure insanity. Two hundred feet up, Farrington waved his hat, blowing kisses to the spectators on both shores. The crowds roared their delight. Cannon on the New York side boomed a salute. I wish you'd been old enough to remember it."

Baxter wanted nothing more than to grow up and build bridges. His father demurred. "Don't waste your time. The Brooklyn Bridge is the masterpiece. The time of the bridgewrights has passed. Now the future is on land, in buildings. Buildings with elevators. You need to study buildings."

When Baxter was seven, his father took him to the corner of Nassau and Beekman where the Potter Building came at them like a red barbarian, iron-framed and insurgent with brick and clay armor, its corner column a lance. "The terra cotta makes it fireproof. Can you believe that? And cheap, too." When Baxter was ten, there was a trip to the Statue of Liberty for its dedication. President Cleveland greeted thousands of spectators. Baxter remembered the smell of autumn and wool outer garments mixed with tobacco. The people strained to hear while staring three hundred feet up to the torch. Cyrus bent to whisper in his son's ear. "All of this should have been ready by the Centennial, but adults can't do anything right."

Baxter giggled and saw stern faces turn toward both of them from above. He felt surrounded by angry trees pressing in. His father fell to a squat and whispered even more quietly, "Don't bother with the statue. It's gaudy, decadent, but what else do you expect from the French? Look at the base instead. That's where the engineering is. That's the important part. It's eighty-nine feet high. Connecticut granite. The openings on the faces are called loggia, and the columns are what kind?"

"Doric," Baxter said. He'd memorized the four basic types. The structure looked to him like a huge chimney chopped off too early and abandoned. He imagined smoke billowing out of it as from a buried locomotive. "There are shields around the bottom."

"Yes, forty of them. They represent each state. Clumsy effort." His father clucked his tongue. "Want to know what I read in the paper? The architect, Richard Morris Hunt, a great man, mind you, says he was inspired by Thomas Jefferson. But Jefferson wanted classical simplicity. Does this look simple to you?"

Baxter took a risk. "It looks ugly."

With gravity, Cyrus placed a hand on his son's back. "I'm afraid so, yes, but we'll forgive it because it's not for decoration. It's instrumental. A good word for you to remember. It means that it has a purpose. The base is not just for show. The statue is made of copper sheets"—he took out a penny—"which is the same as what this is made of." The penny was warm when his father put it into his hand. "But those sheets are on an iron frame which sinks all the way into the base. That's why it's so strong. That's why it won't blow over in a storm."

A statue made of pennies, Baxter thought.

Always new buildings to see. They watched foundations get dug, piles driven, steel fastened and set climbing. At night, outside the

Vanderbilt chateau on Fifth Avenue and 52nd, they stood before the intermittently lighted windows in the pale limestone, four stories so different from the dirty brownstones of old New York. Instead of a tall stoop, a wide flight of shallow steps. The arch above the entrance opened from a wall adorned with ogee moldings and nooks. A slender turret with fleurs-de-lis and a high blue slate roof with copper crestings and finials. "Now *this* is a house," Cyrus said.

"I wonder what it looks like inside."

"I can't get us that far. You'll have to work your own way inside."

"Who designed it?"

"Richard Morris Hunt again. I tell you, the man is a genius. You remember when we went to the Museum of Art? That's his, too. He got the idea for the design from the French Ministry of Justice, and that's exactly what he's bringing to the public. This country isn't a backwoods sumpwater anymore. It's growing up! It should be proud of itself! When you study in college, you'll see. You'll have your own ideas and make them great."

Cyrus taught him to draft. When Baxter was sixteen, a design of his for a children's library won a contest for amateur artists and, by his seventeenth birthday, the portfolio he'd sent to schools was being well received. He hadn't yet been rejected from the 10th Street Studio, Hunt's own school. Bad luck to hope that he'd have the opportunity to study with the great man himself.

But the hope was fulfilled. His acceptance letter arrived in May. He could begin at Hunt's studio in August. He ran to the study.

"I got in!"

No reaction. Newspapers were strewn about. At first glance, Cyrus appeared to be reading. His posture was bent, his spectacles in place. His head was oddly lifted. He was not reading. He was staring at the wall.

Baxter moved forward with unease. "Did you hear what I said? I'm going to study with Hunt."

The warmth in the bearded face that turned toward him, its vulnerability, frightened him. In Cyrus' eyes, he'd never seen tears. "That's wonderful. I'm very proud of you." He pulled his son close and embraced him. "I knew you could do it. But I'm sorry. I'm so sorry." He quaked with sobs.

1893.

The Panic.

~

Cyrus was left with only his job. The house was lost. They moved to a small apartment in Brooklyn. The investments Cyrus made to pay for Baxter's schooling were obliterated. Railroad and cordage companies had performed strongly before the plummet. "It's over," Cyrus said. "I bought rope and they hung me with it."

As to Baxter's own devastated hopes, he tried his best to conceal them. The Panic aged his father. Gray hairs conquered his head and beard. Flickers of insouciance fled his eyes. Reticence began a slow eviction of his voice, and Cyrus rose for work sluggishly, moving along like a soft tire. In order not to add to his father's humiliation and pain, Baxter swallowed his own ambitions and cast about for practicality. He found a job as a page at the stock exchange, enrolled in City College for the fall semester.

"You might have to pay for those classes yourself, son. I don't think I'll be able to help you, but I will if I can, of course."

"I'll go slow. I'll take on what I can. I'm only seventeen, father. I'll make it through. Don't worry. I'll be fine. *We'll* be fine."

During his first semester, Baxter registered only for a preliminary accounting class to see if he could handle the work along with his job. In his second semester, he increased his course load to two classes, adding one in management. He settled into this pace and crawled toward his degree.

Meanwhile, the market roiled. Because he wanted to speak intelligently with the traders about what drove their decisions, Baxter began to read the papers in earnest. A riptide of gold fled offshore as thousands of banks melted away. Engines stopped on one-third of all the railroads, and the plunge hardened into a depression which scraped across the country like a rough flint sparking fires.

Coxey's Army of unemployed marched from Ohio to D.C. for jobs and public works, only to be arrested for trampling the Capitol's grass. In the Midwest, Pullman warred against Debs and his membership, and railroad ties became sticks of dynamite. In Pennsylvania and Ohio, much the same. Eastern coal took to light. Sometime in the middle of Baxter's junior year, twelve-thousand garment workers walked off the job just blocks from where he sat.

He saw nothing first-hand. It all came to him in print. A segregating experience, to have a regular job and regular duties. Routine somehow kept the world at bay. He needed to turn in assignments, pass messages on the trading floor. He learned and even enjoyed his classics, wrote up his case studies. His tasks required completion yesterday and would again tomorrow. The world outside would have to take care of itself for the time being. He was occupied with survival. The alternative was not pleasant to contemplate. He thought of his father, who dragged now from year to year. Age does not battle well with disappointment. Baxter was thankful for his youth.

She spoke to him first, at registration time at college. "By my count, this is your fifth year. Not progressing too quickly, are we?"

He stopped his paperwork. The shine of her eyes. The plainness of the parted black hair that swept to the top of her head. He considered his response. Her cheeks flushed red. He felt the warmth from her soft, youth-rounded features. "What's your name?"

"Lorraine."

"I'll have you know, Lorraine, that I'm studying as hard as I can."

"But not too quickly."

He lowered his pen at her forwardness, playful all the same. "And what if there were another reason for my pace?"

"Such as?"

"I have to work while I study. My family lost everything in the Panic."

"Are you joking?"

"I wouldn't joke about that."

"My goodness, I'm sorry." She reached for his hand. "I was only teasing."

"I don't know if I can forgive you. We should walk together and discuss this."

In a year they were in love and there was war with Spain. The Ivins Syndicate Building went up on Park Row. In one of its copper-clad domes, thirty stories above the street, Baxter proposed, and graduation brought an offer from Mr. Robertson's company.

"Doing what?"

"Accounting at first. It's a good start. I can move into management after a few years."

He remembered thinking, *I am an adult now.* His father's voice from before the Panic had not completely disappeared. "You could be a great man someday, Harlan, and great men shape the world." A voice that spoke from conditions long ago erased. Responsibility impended. Time and experience had made Baxter cautious and a technician. If he could not be a great man, he could at least work for one. A stable income wasn't the worst fate.

Sadness thickened his throat. The first time his father had seen Thomas sleeping, life and color returned to his face. Baxter and Lorraine stood by as Cyrus looked into the cradle.

"He's a beautiful child, simply beautiful," Cyrus whispered.

Lorraine said, "You must hold him."

"No, no, don't disturb him."

"Nonsense." With quick delicacy, she lifted the baby. Thomas did not stir.

In a rocking chair, Cyrus sat with the baby. With great tenderness he brushed his thumb across Thomas' forehead.

"Whenever you like, just lay him back down," Lorraine said. She kissed Cyrus on the cheek, urged Baxter from the room, closed the door. "Did you see his face?" she said.

"Yes. Peaceful."

In the cell he blinked away tears. *Dead now. Everyone in my memory. Come back. Please, come back, Lorraine. The dark green lust of Central Park in the summer was not so long ago. Come back, father. We'll talk before buildings again, under bridges again. Come back, Thomas. Claim the life that was robbed from you. Come back, all. What I long for. My decisions to have been correct. For time to fill its bowl more slowly. For lives to progress to their natural ends.*

14

His stomach went heavy at the sight of the weapons.

"Maybe think twice before you accuse me of disobeying orders."

"I was out of line," Baxter said. "I should have given you the benefit of the doubt."

"What do you want to do?"

Baxter closed the crate, trying to sort his emotions and think clearly. "Is this the extent of their supply?"

"Don't know, but I doubt it. Like I said, these are just the ones we know about. I'd sure like to get into that camp to look for more, though."

Baxter considered the idea for a moment, almost swayed. "No. Let's wait on that. It would be too provocative. If we go smashing through their things with just the wives and children around, there won't be any talking to them. We've had our show of force. We'll keep the men inside for a few days to teach them a lesson."

"They'll be even more riled when they're released."

"Maybe not, provided we give them decent food, water, and rotate them out to relieve themselves."

Unresponsive, Lind replaced the padlock on the crate.

"Mr. Lind, did you hear me? Food, water, and relief."

"Yes, sir."

"And no violence."

"I can't promise that. Might have to use it for self-defense."

"Don't provoke them, and you won't have to defend yourself."

"Yes, sir. I guess that's right, sir."

Baxter climbed down from the boxcar. "I don't want to see these guns again."

"What should we do with them?"

"Bury them. Burn them. I don't care. Just make sure they disappear."

Lind jumped to the ground. "I'll take you back to town."

"Don't bother. The exercise will do me good."

A chill had settled into the afternoon air, and the stovepipes among the tents smoked into a late-November sky. At the edge of the camp, Baxter paused, steadying himself. He was apprehensive at entering unannounced and unescorted, but he could think of no alternative. He needed a reliable interlocutor, and somewhere in these tents was the only possible candidate.

As he walked through the camp, searching, women in the rows worked at laundry and cooking, here and there conversing in pairs. If they noticed him, they fell silent, wary and confused as he passed. They averted their eyes and turned their backs, dedicating every movement to ignoring him. The men who had escaped arrest reacted more fiercely to his presence, abandoning their smithing or tent repairs and facing him directly with crossed arms. Baxter felt the heat of their hostility. Before long he was lost. This was no way to find anyone. He realized he'd have to ask for help.

He approached a man on his knees by a tent. Hammer blows on plank flooring rang out. Baxter's presence made the hammer fall idle, but the man did not release it.

Baxter said, "I need to find Mr. Chamm."

The man regarded him for a long moment, out of incomprehension or stonewalling or for some other reason, Baxter didn't know. Laying the hammer down, the man stood up and wiped his hands on his pants. He bested Baxter's height by several inches.

Baxter tried again. "I need to see Mr. Chamm."

This time the man pointed to a tent on the perimeter nearest to the street. With relief, Baxter walked where directed and knocked on the main support pole.

Chamm's voice came from inside. "Yeah?"

Baxter pushed the canvas aside. The tent was illuminated by candles that flickered under the breeze of the just-opened fly. On three empty crates, Chamm, Anna, and a small boy sat near an iron stove.

"Baxter," Chamm said.

"I ain't apologizin' for tossin' that egg at you," Anna said.

"Hush," Chamm said. He stood and squared himself. "Well?"

Where to begin? Baxter thought. Guns? Violence? Duplicity? No. Keep to the task at hand. "I want to talk to you about the men in jail."

"No doubt." Chamm beckoned for Anna and the boy to stand.

Baxter said, "You don't have to leave."

"Relax," Chamm said.

They pushed the crates to the edge of the flooring, and Chamm drew aside a ratty burlap rug. He lifted a trap door to reveal a hole in the dirt. Chamm dropped down, and Baxter peered into the makeshift basement. "Dug these after the tents went up," Chamm said from below, rooting around. "Good for storin'. Cooler in the summers, too." He handed up a short stool made from scrap logs. "Somethin' for you to set on."

Baxter thanked him and helped him from the hole. With the trap closed and the rug replaced, everyone sat down again. Near the stove, Baxter felt a little more at ease.

"This here's Oliver," Chamm said, laying a hand on the boy's shoulder.

"It's nice to meet you," Baxter said.

Shy, Oliver dropped his head.

"Go on," Anna said, "Show your manners."

"It's nice to meet you, too, sir."

"I have a son about your age."

"We could play together."

"I think he'd like that."

"But don't count on it, right?" Chamm said, watching Baxter.

Baxter looked at the boy and then back at Chamm. "There's no need to drag our children into our affairs."

"That's on point." Chamm lit a cigarette and patted Oliver's leg. "Boss man's right for once. How about that?"

"State your business, Mr. Baxter," Anna said. "We all got chores need doing."

"Yes, well, it's simple, really," Baxter said. "I ordered humane treatment for those fellows in jail, and I need someone to make sure they receive it."

"What's that got to do with me?"

"I'd like you to make sure for me."

"That don't make sense. Lind's your man," Chamm said. Then he relaxed with sudden understanding. "Huh. Times is hard in the coalfields, ain't they, Baxter?"

"They've been better," Baxter said.

"What?" Anna said.

"He can't trust his own man. He thinks Lind is snakin' him."

No worse than you did with those rifles, Baxter thought. "Not exactly. It's hard to explain."

"Why don't you do your own checking?"

"When I'm around, everyone's always on their best behavior."

Anna scoffed.

"I mean, it's hard for me to get the truth, but it won't be for you. You have a network. People talk to you."

"I ain't your snitch."

"I only want to know about conditions."

"How about something on our end?"

"Like what?"

"Tell me how long they'll be inside."

Baxter pulled a number from the air. "If you say nothing to them about it, I promise they'll be out in three days, provided they behave."

"We can deal on that."

"Just tell me whether they're being fed or if the guards are kicking the hell out of them."

"Don't worry. I'll shoot you straight."

~

Baxter went to the jail each day for the next two days. Everything appeared to be in order. The men were groggy, tired, and ornery, but since he'd heard nothing from Chamm, he was confident his instructions were being heeded. On each visit, Hawkins tried to draw him into debate. Each time, Baxter begged off conversation, giving no hints as to when the imprisonment might end.

On the night preceding the men's release, and with Baxter's authorization, Lind turned on the searchlights. Outside his house, Baxter stood in the street and watched the beams crawl in a slow pattern over the camp. The thin walls of the tents would do little to snuff the light. Chamm and the others would have difficulty sleeping, but Baxter concurred with Lind now. The lights were useful. The company could not let its charges doubt its authority.

He climbed to the porch and sat down in one of the wicker chairs. The cold was intensifying daily. In the morning, frost might appear on the sage. Lorraine, in her night clothes, opened the front door.

"Harlan, it's late," she said. "Time for bed."

"I know."

She ducked into the house and reappeared wearing her own coat. She sat down beside him. Baxter took her hand. "He has a son."

"Who?"

"Chamm. He's got a boy about Thomas' age."

"You don't say."

Baxter bowed his head. "It's going to get worse for them, you know."

"I thought you were going to release the men tomorrow."

"I am. I will. But the strike has already lasted too long."

"You're trying your best."

Baxter sniffed. "So far I've been sharp enough to get myself arrested with the only negotiator in town."

"You haven't talked to him yet?"

"Not seriously. It's impossible while he's in jail."

"He has to learn his lesson along with the rest."

"Still and all, the company needs to fulfill its orders."

She watched him until she saw clearly. "Scabs."

"We call them replacement workers. We've already wired a request."

"What happens when they arrive?"

"I don't know, but perhaps you and Thomas should go back to New York."

"By ourselves? Why?"

"It would be safer."

"How are things different now than when we arrived?"

He hadn't told her about the boxcar. He still hesitated to do so, seeing little purpose in stressing her about a situation she was powerless to change. But he didn't want to lie to her either. "We found a cache of weapons."

"Where?"

"On one of the union trains. They were hidden in some supplies."

"What did you do with them?"

"Seized them, locked them away. I ordered Lind to destroy them."

"And were those all?"

"That's exactly what I asked."

She turned a stern face toward him.

"The truth is we don't know. Lind isn't sure. The only other place to hide weapons would be in the tents, and Chamm, if he's at all representative of the miners, doesn't strike me as stupid enough to hide weapons in the first place we'd look for them."

"Then I don't see any reason to leave."

"Lorraine."

"There's danger everywhere, Harlan. We can't just run away at the slightest disturbance. Who knows, on our way home we could be hurt in a train accident, and then think of how silly you'd feel." She squeezed his hand. "It's cold," she said. "And Thomas is asleep."

They crept up the stairs and into their bedroom.

At first, Baxter only followed. Motivated more by the others' momentum than by his own volition, he was aware of his actions but from a mute distance.

The young Norwegian whose name he could not remember volunteered to go north and destroy the tracks to town. The tortuous, four-way translation. The Norwegian spoke French to another man who also spoke German, who spoke German to another who spoke Italian, who spoke Italian to a last who spoke pained and fractured English. Without dirt in which to draw with their fingers, they would have been lost.

The Norwegian was accustomed to snow. He had grown up north of the Arctic Circle. He knew how to read drifts and wind. He was no more afraid of night, cold, solitude, and silence than he was of clean air. He agreed with the decision to fight, admitted to physical cowardice. He worked with other men because life required it, but he preferred to work alone.

Sabotage for him, then.

They scrounged amongst themselves for extra clothes, manufactured a backpack from scrap wire and burlap. Into the pack: black powder, a few fuses and empty cans, a large bag of lentils. The snow now deep on the plain. The only time of year when the high desert held water. The Norwegian asked for eight days. In that time, he might reach the midpoint to Denver, explode the rails. The most remote location. The most difficult for repairs. Success would mean a long delay of troops.

Failure? A few wounds inflicted before the end. Eight days, then fight. The Norwegian headed for the westernmost tunnel and disappeared.

Consider the old man. He might favor severed tracks. Let the locals smash away at each other for a while. Let time curve out like a scythe. Wait and see, weigh options according to circumstances, choose tactics to preserve the investment. The most deliberate man Baxter had ever heard of.

Through the wait, they used a large stope as their common room and a distant tunnel for relieving themselves. They moved bags of beans to a stope near the spring and hoped, because they could do little else, that when they boiled water in an upturned helmet, methane didn't find the flames.

They sat in the common room and fed sounds to the darkness, drawings to the dirt. Stories emerged by erosion in reverse. A stone formed, rolled away. In its place another accreted. Baxter tried with all his strength to listen, to understand.

15

The next afternoon, Lind and Baxter opened the cell. Weary, the men exited with decorum and only a few hate-filled glances toward Lind. Hawkins emerged last and stood at ease as Lind locked the now-empty cell.

"Enjoy your stay?" Lind asked him.

Hawkins turned ostentatiously toward Baxter. "I don't mind if *you* visit me, but leave your dog at home next time. I'm allergic."

Lind tossed the keys aside to fight, but Baxter stopped him, grabbing him lightly by the elbow.

"Baxter, I'm begging you," Lind said.

"Control yourself."

"Indeed," Hawkins said.

"You, too," Baxter said. "We're even, Mr. Hawkins. You saved me a beating. Now I've done the same for you. My debt is paid."

Lind moved into the booking room while Hawkins watched him go. Baxter felt the room fill with silence.

"We need to talk," Baxter said.

"Surely. Tonight. But I need to confer with Mr. Chamm first. Come to his tent around eight."

"That's not a suitable place for discussion."

"Just be there. We'll figure out someplace else then if you like."

Baxter agreed and departed for the post office, where he collected two telegrams. The company's subcontractor in Chicago reported that replacement workers were being recruited and would arrive sometime the following week. Baxter preferred precise delivery estimates, but at least he now wielded a solid threat against the strikers. If they saw that the company was prepared to continue on without them, they might give up their effort.

The second telegram troubled him. In the course of his investigations, Baxter had stumbled on a state-sponsored study of the mine complex. The study was a few years old by the time Baxter found it, but he considered its information relevant enough to incorporate into his report. The study compared the safety record of the company's closed camps to unionized camps under different ownership elsewhere in the state. The former came off terribly. He informed the old man but had not requested a response. Evidently, Mr. Robertson had been moved to supply one anyway.

> REGARDING SAFETY COMPARISON STOP ENOUGH NONSENSE
> STOP LIND AND YOU CAN SOLVE IT STOP FULL CONFIDENCE
> IN ABILITIES STOP
>
> P.D.R.

Nonsense? The word was disturbing, calling into question Baxter's approach. After all, if the company's comparative safety record wasn't worthy of Mr. Robertson's attention, what else might fall beneath his interest? Baxter had to think more carefully about the information he conveyed in the future, which only made him feel more alone.

~

He arrived as promised at Chamm's tent. The talks then moved to the saloon, to the rear of it, to a supply room for which Chamm retained a key. Baxter and Hawkins and Chamm all entered from the alley side. Surrounded by shelves of canned food and liquor locked behind wire-screened cabinets, a card table bore the scattered hands of a defunct game.

Baxter and Chamm sat down. Hawkins passed through an adjoining door. No sound spilled from the drinking parlor. The silence was unnerving, unnatural. Baxter had been in the saloon when the men were drawing scrip. Lively, raucous sounds should fill the building, not a dead, near-vacuum.

Hawkins returned with a half empty bottle of whiskey and two shot glasses. He poured three fingers of liquor into each glass, draining his own in one gulp. Baxter matched Hawkins' shot and pushed the glass forward for a refill. Hawkins did not immediately oblige him.

"We've got big problems, Mr. Baxter," Hawkins said.

"I hardly think that's my fault."

"You could recognize the union," Chamm said. "Wouldn't be no problems then."

"And you could call off the strike."

"We could do that," Hawkins said. "But we did that the first three times."

"This is the fourth strike?"

Hawkins drummed his fingers on the table. He'd purged his eyes of mirth. "It's the seventh strike, Baxter, but the first of substantial duration. The others were much smaller and only lasted a day or two each. Quite frankly, I'm amazed you don't know that already."

Now Hawkins refilled Baxter's glass, but Baxter did not drink immediately. He wanted to figure out a response beforehand. Each strike might have generated a memo to the heads of the relevant divisions. On the other hand, if the strikes were small, they might have passed without mention. The New York office consumed so much paperwork that the glossing over of two-day strikes was entirely plausible. Nevertheless, he should have known. He opted for honesty. "I didn't have time to do my usual preliminaries. I had to leave New York too quickly." He felt the inadequacy of the words as he said them.

Hawkins leaned back in his chair. "After each strike we took our grievances through the usual channels, the labor boards and such, and each time, the governor and the company did nothing."

"There are other avenues. Lawsuits, for instance."

"The laws are already on the books. There's no enforcement."

Baxter drank again, abstemiously this time.

"They keep us separated," Chamm said. "No Italians working with Italians. No Greeks with Greeks. Ain't too many men like me with the gift, so most ways nobody talks to nobody else."

"Isolation," Hawkins added. "Divide and conquer."

Baxter did not respond. He believed what he was hearing, but the strike had to end before he could do anything significant. "I can increase the rate you're paid for tonnage. Mr. Robertson is also amenable to a payment for dead work."

"He said that?" Chamm asked.

"He's considering it."

Chamm snorted and turned away.

Hawkins said, "Let's entertain for the sake of argument that such an increase is granted. How much are we talking about?"

"I'd say about five percent for the tonnage increase, and maybe a dollar or three weekly for dead work."

Chamm laughed once.

"And unionization?" Hawkins asked.

"Out of the question."

"Naturally," Hawkins said. He stood and paced for a moment. He picked up a can of beans, rotated it, and placed it back on the shelf.

"I want you to know," Baxter said, "that I've been completely honest in the reports I've cabled back."

"I'm sure you have," Hawkins said.

"And you're insinuating what?"

"Nothing at all. I believe you. But honest answers can be quite irrelevant, you know, especially when you're not asking the right questions."

"Such as?"

"Why would one of the most powerful and savvy men in the world send an accountant to defuse a strike?"

"It's been a long time since I was just his accountant. Plus, there wasn't a strike when I was sent. I came here on a fact-finding mission. The strike began after I arrived. Don't rewrite the past."

Hawkins waved his hand dismissively. "The strike was entirely foreseeable. Robertson knew it, and he sent you anyway. Surely he employs people more qualified than you for this sort of thing."

"He has a great deal of trust in me."

Hawkins' face hardened again. He turned to Chamm. "You sure weren't kidding."

"I told you," Chamm said. "Green as a spring leaf."

"Now, look," Baxter said.

"It's true, Mr. Baxter," Chamm said gingerly.

"It's *false*. I've got experience."

"In negotiating strikes?" Hawkins said.

"In fixing problems. I can't count the number of projects Mr. Robertson has brought me in on over the years. Whenever there's been a situation requiring special, delicate attention, I've been called. He can't attend personally to everything that happens in his company."

"And you think you're the only man on call for his special projects? You think you're indispensable?"

Baxter huffed from his chair and circled to a corner as if to trap his anger there.

Chamm said to him, "Remember when you came to see us during the ball game? Remember when you first tried to talk with us?"

"Yes," Baxter said.

"Ever figure what the batter said?"

"I haven't the foggiest. I don't speak Italian."

"He said he was going to knock your fucking head off. And he would have, too. He called you a piece of shit."

"Is that so?"

"You stirred him up good."

Hawkins sat down again. He said, "Join me at the table, Baxter. Please. There's something I need to tell you."

Seated again, Baxter finished his drink. Hawkins leaned toward him. "You're window dressing, Baxter. Good public relations. If any of the papers sniff out a major strike, Robertson tells them he transferred one of his senior fixers to handle the situation. He omits the fact that said fixer is totally unfit for the task."

Baxter grew warm with indignation.

"Think about it," Hawkins continued. "How much sway have you had with Lind? I mean, yes, you've taken the edge off of him somewhat. We appreciated your solicitude in jail. But fundamentally speaking, has your word had any influence at all? Has company policy changed one iota because of your role?"

"My opinion carries considerable weight with the company. And I can tell you for certain that I'm not favorably disposed toward threats."

"Threats?" Hawkins said. "Mr. Baxter, this is *courtesy*."

Chamm asked, "When are the scabs comin'?"

"They don't have to come at all if you go back to work."

"When?" Hawkins said sharply.

"I don't know."

"You can't possibly expect us to believe that," Hawkins said. "If you tell us, it'll be safer for everyone."

"Some are coming, but I don't know exactly when." He rested his hands, one on each side of the shot glass, index fingers touching as if in preparation for prayer. The men had been idle for too many weeks, and his highest concern was for the mine to resume operation. He was not sure whether to play his trump, but the time did seem ripe, so he laid it down. "It's a bit hypocritical for you to be talking about safety."

"How's that?" Hawkins said.

"I saw those guns."

"What guns?"

"Don't be coy. Lind took me out to the boxcar and showed them to me. Dressing them up as supplies was clever."

"By any chance would this have been about the time your extra goons arrived?"

"More or less."

"And the weapons you saw—were they shiny? Did they look new?"

"Yes."

"They looked like military issue, didn't they? Just the kind of equipment a well-financed security company would use, correct?"

Dread swept into him. "Yes," Baxter said again.

"Well," Hawkins continued, "I don't know what Lind showed you, but I can promise you that no union has the resources to buy weapons like that." He poured another drink for himself and for Baxter. "You're a fool, sir." He raised his glass. "You're a nice enough man on your own merits, but you are unquestionably a fool."

They sat in silence for a long time. An incongruous feeling of calm came over Baxter. He'd felt more pity than condemnation in Hawkins' rebuke, and he could not understand how having his own stupidity exposed had somehow smoothed the situation. Perhaps the lifting of pretense had done it. Baxter bowed his head, pillowing it in his hands. He rubbed at his eyes. His skull felt ponderously heavy. "I don't know what to think anymore," he murmured.

As Chamm went to answer a knock at the door, he said, "Just tell the company we're not rolling over this time."

Anna entered with Oliver's hand in her own. "Best come on back," she said. "They're at it again."

They ran back to camp. The air sounded of shrill whistles and hoofbeats. Snow flurries had commenced. Baxter felt the impact of flakes on his face as he ran. Men and horses were tearing through the strikers' colony, ripping open the tents and tossing out the contents. Books, pots, and clothes littered the ground amid the seething strikers and their wives. In the chaos, one horse passed so close to Baxter that it knocked him down. He shot to his feet again, enraged, and when another horse swept near, he grabbed its reins and yanked down. The horse wheeled. The man atop it rose up with a club, but Baxter's previous arrest had made him known, and the man stayed his hand.

"What the hell is going on?" Baxter demanded.

"Searchin' the tents, sir. We got another report about weapons."

Disgusted, Baxter released the reins and withdrew, helpless. Strikers poured out of the tents, fleeing to the camp perimeter, standing in groups as the guards tossed their lives onto the dirt, measled now with snow.

Baxter could barely bring himself to watch. Lind's brazenness was inestimable. Baxter expected at any moment to hear gunfire erupt. He kept glancing up and then dropping his head again. He ground his teeth as Hawkins whispered to him, "Do you see? Do you see?"

The scouts at the driftmouths waited for the tent fires to diminish. Retreat. Gather. Discuss the path forward. Fight or yield. Baxter said, "Chamm would want us to fight." Us, he thought.

"Hell, yes," Pierce said.

Garris, surefooted, cautious, asked for another confirmation. Baxter did not reverse himself.

They made their decisions by sitting down behind the pistol or walking away from it. To those who chose not to join, Garris instructed, "Tell 'em we all dead. Tell 'em that. They won't believe you, but they won't come in here neither. Tell 'em anything for time."

From the driftmouths marched columns of women, men, and children, arms raised, moving toward the plain, past the graves already dug, toward the train for what might be safe passage.

Within the earth, deliberation and slow preparation. The Norwegian made his proposal, and planning commenced. Baxter, numb as a stone, followed.

Like abandoned carcasses, broken and overturned carts populated the tunnels, carts that had never been removed for repairs, merely hauled aside where they wouldn't obstruct work. Beneath those carts lay sacks of lentils, boxes of ammunition. A weapon here, a brick of hard-tack there. Dried pasta secreted in crevices. Threadbare clothing and hanks of fuses behind boulders. Under one track tie, fifteen pistols. Under another, ten bottles of whiskey.

The men moved about, unpacking. Incredible logistics. Baxter asked when the hoarding had begun. "Since the last strike. A year," Garris said. All of it undetected. The company never bothered to search the tunnels for contraband. Too difficult, too dangerous. As long as the men brought up the coal, the company ignored the tunnels. From time to time the miners themselves planted contraband in their own housing for Lind to find. To make him think they were too stupid to hide it elsewhere. Garris said, "This is how you do, Baxter. A little at a time. Ain't a limit to what can get done then. Time can build. You just have to give it a chance."

Baxter marveled. The quantities! Supplies stashed throughout the complex. He hadn't thought it possible to accomplish so much so slowly. As to wisdom, as to whether the plans might end in folly, No concern of mine, he thought. I have lost everything. I am without hope. I will act and act and act and that itself will suffice. From now on, I will think with my blood.

He had not seen water among the supplies. He scraped his tongue along the inside of his mouth, rough as a dry sponge. Someone led him to the spring at the end of a deep tunnel, played-out but not sealed, a hot tunnel. Water dripped from the ceiling and formed a small pool on the floor. Baxter's thirst sprang from its cage, yet he was careful not to stir the sediment when he cupped his hands to drink. The water tasted clean and sweet. The spring would supply enough for fifty men, maybe more.

Lind might already be prepared.

Lind might not be prepared at all.

16

Baxter skulked home, hobbled by anger and sapped by shame. Lind had not shown his face during the search. Holed up in the tipple, no doubt. Hiding. Baxter felt too done-in to chase him down. The snow was falling harder, and he was cold.

He fell into bed. Through a fitful sleep he dreamed of the morning he'd received news of his transfer. He'd been released early from his duties and had entered the lunchtime currents of suited men on Wall Street. He pushed for space among the bowlers and dark jackets, not accustomed to negotiating crowds at that time of day. Usually he took his lunch alone in his office, considering it a waste of time to descend to street level just to eat and re-ascend. Again, he walked beneath the thatch of telegraph wire twenty feet above his head. Again, he felt a sense of foreboding. The lines collapsed often, and now with phone wires being added to them, the office would endure further interruptions.

The warmth of the day, not stifling, but hot enough that he removed his jacket as he stopped under the striped awning of a cigar store. He was not a regular smoker, and since he did not want to convey an air of celebration, he resolved to finish the cigar before arriving home.

In the counters, all the boxes lay open with gaudy and colorful drawings on the undersides of their lids. The store was redolent of tobacco. He inhaled and lingered before the most expensive brands, thinking that a small salute might indeed be justified. After all, Mr. Robertson's picking him for the assignment indicated a substantial amount of trust. A fine point alongside the relocation issue? He bought a mid-range cigar and a copy of the *Metropolitan* to read by the piers. He paused streetside to punch a hole in the cigar with a key. He cupped his hands over the match to light it, puffed a few times, and got on his way.

Soon, he smelled the river again. Rank humidity prowled the streets of the lower East Side, the air a mixture of fresh fish, moisture, smoke, and commerce. At South Street the water came into view, calm in cells between the piers and roiling with tidal whitecaps farther out. With the paper in his lap, he sat on an empty bench at the foot of a nearby dock.

Standard for the front page. News from the Mexican revolution and the Chinese civil war. Debate continued over Owen-Glass and the establishment of a federal reserve system. He flipped through the pages, skimming for a particular item. HENRY KENDALL THAW ESCAPES FROM MATTEAWAN and FUSION TICKET OF REPUBLICANS and GOVERNOR SULZER STRUGGLES BEFORE FRAWLEY INQUIRY. He stopped. Section D, page thirty-five, a two-inch article in the bottom right-hand corner. MINE ACCIDENT IN COLORADO. Hardly more than a tally of the dead and the name of the town. An insignificant, buried article. Little threat to the company. He was pleased not to be diving into a cauldron of publicity.

Focus on practicalities. Take winter clothes and leave the formal apparel in Brooklyn. Pack with speed and as much convenience as possible. Think how the boy would probably enjoy the trip most. Not good for a boy to grow up completely in a city, forays to Central Park notwithstanding. Thomas ought to see a little of the country. Baxter pulled his hat down against a gust of East River wind. He traversed the bridge, reaching the middle of the promenade above the roadway traffic. He paused to enjoy the view and the last of his cigar. Far below, steam tugs moved about their usual work in puffs of white. Fishing schooners docked at the piers to the southwest. The river frothed with wind and an ebbing tide beneath a sky of shattering blue.

~

Two feet of accumulation met him outside in the morning. Two feet of snow in a desert, no less, he thought. Nothing to do but push through it. On his way to the office, he passed the tent colony, now in shambles. The search and the weight of the snow had flattened the tents. The strikers and their families crawled about, salvaging what they could. Baxter saw Hawkins rise from a stoop and stretch his back. Baxter turned quickly, hoping to avoid notice.

"That's right, Baxter!" Hawkins yelled, his voice just audible over the distance. "Walk on by! It's always easier to walk on by!"

Baxter wished for a blast of wind to carry away the words. He slogged to town, looking for Lind. He could not find him. He thought briefly about continuing to the tipple, but he was not sure how out of control Lind was, so he tasked one of the mounted guards with delivering a message: Mr. Lind should report to town. Lind's acceptance or refusal of the summons would say quite a lot.

Lind arrived as demanded. Baxter waited for him in the mine office. Lind stood before the desk, jaw clamped, simultaneously angry at having been fetched, yet obedient for the moment before authority.

Baxter said, "Tell me something, Mr. Lind. How is it that as the company's security chief you're succeeding at little but *decreasing* security? Have you thought about what's going to happen when those people decide to fight back?"

"My men are prepared for that."

"That's what we're trying to prevent!"

Lind wouldn't meet his eyes, which Baxter didn't interpret as shame but rather as a posture of barely maintained submission. He wondered how long Lind's deference to power could hold out against his desire to rebel.

"The search was unconscionable," Baxter continued. "That camp is a powder keg, and you sent your men in to throw matches. You endangered everyone here, not to mention the company and its assets."

"We had another report about guns. The information was solid."

That's a lie, Baxter thought, a bald-faced lie. Give me one shred of truth to hang on to. "And did you find anything?"

Lind said nothing.

"Answer me."

"A pistol or two."

"Which wasn't worth the risk."

"You'd prefer we found more?"

"I'd prefer you come to me first. In fact, I ordered you to do so. Have you forgotten the whole purpose of my being here?"

"I really don't know what your purpose is here, sir."

Baxter was not shaken. He had been expecting this moment and seized on it, leaning in close and glaring at Lind so as to show he was not intimidated. "Be careful, Mr. Lind. Don't ever forget your place. I am Paul David Robertson's eyes and ears in this valley, and as such, I will be obeyed. We are to work together for the good of the company, but cross me again, and I'll have your job."

Lind stewed in place. "Is that all?"

"No. You and your men are to stay out of town for the day. The farther away from camp, the better."

Lind waited in silence.

"Now you may go," Baxter said.

Lind left, maybe without his tail sufficiently between his legs but chastened enough for Baxter's satisfaction. He thought, One foul task addressed. He put on his overcoat to address the second.

Close up, the reclamation disconcerted him more greatly than he expected. Because the men had downed their tools at the start of the strike, they hadn't any shovels. People were digging out their tents with pots and pans or simply with their ungloved hands. They'd cleared pathways wide enough to walk down, but for the most part the camp remained collapsed and smothered.

At the sight of Baxter, Hawkins stopped digging. Sweating, his body steamed like an oxen's into the frigid afternoon. "Astounding," Hawkins panted. "To just stride in here like nothing's happened? You are truly a man with no shame."

"I'm not in the mood for any of your rubbish right now," Baxter warned. "This is not my fault. Do you hear me? This is not my fault."

"I wish I had your nerve. I could have beaten Amundsen to the South Pole."

Baxter didn't want to waste any more energy arguing. He turned about and yelled. "I'm sorry this happened!"

Across the camp, backs straightened and hands fell idle. The strikers watched him. The background of endless white plain robbed him momentarily of his voice. He felt as if he'd stumbled into a feudal village on the Russian steppe. "I'm sorry about all this," he said. "You cannot imagine how sorry. Rest assured, I've disciplined Mr. Lind. That's all I can do at the moment other than help you clean up. If anyone objects, I'll leave, but it looks like you need all the help you can get."

For a long time, he waited for a reaction. He had never felt so watched. Eyes held him like an arrested man. Then, something hit him hard from behind. He stumbled and fell into the snow. When he righted himself, a large iron pot lay at his feet. Chamm's voice came to him. "Time for another shift, boss man."

Baxter picked up the pot and started digging.

"Absolutely astounding," Hawkins muttered, scooping again at the snow.

The others followed suit. First, they cleared entrances to the tents, then they propped up the canvases, the snow sloughing off in heavy, muffled thuds. The pathways never grew much wider but did eventually link into a network for foot traffic among the tents. As darkness fell, Baxter realized with bitterness that the searchlights would allow everyone to work well into the night if they desired, yet his energy evaporated as the moon edged over the western ridge. His clothes hung heavy with sweat and melted snow. He handed his pot to the man working beside him and trudged for home. No one acknowledged his departure.

~

At the house he stripped down to his shorts and undershirt. Just inside the front door, his clothes fell with wet slaps into a heap. He'd only brought one overcoat to Colorado, and since he would need it again the following morning, Lorraine hung it by the fire. He went upstairs and changed into dry garments before he caught a chill. He put on his robe and returned to the kitchen, where he poured himself a large drink.

"I'll fix you dinner if you like," Lorraine said.

"Just put some water on for me. Oatmeal will do."

"For dinner? And after whiskey? That's revolting."

"Believe me, I'm too tired to taste anything."

She loaded kindling into the burner and clanked down a pot for boiling. "Did you look in on Thomas?"

"He's reading," Baxter said. "I just said hello. I didn't want to interrupt."

"He wonders where his father has been lately."

"I'll make it up to him in New York," Baxter said. He didn't need to be reminded of his duty to his family, nor of his neglect of it. "I butted heads with Lind today."

"Did you win?"

"I think so."

"After what he did last night, you should have fired him."

"No question."

"Why didn't you?"

He went to his overcoat and took out the telegram about the replacement workers. Lorraine read it with vexation. "If you can't trust him, Lind won't do you any good when these men arrive."

"I'd rather have shaky security than none at all." His undiminished sense of dependence on Lind disgusted him. He felt aimless with fatigue. His thoughts drifted. Nevertheless, he felt the need to talk. For no particular reason, he said, "Seven miners in this state are killed per every thousand. That's twice the national average, and four times Illinois, Iowa, and Missouri, where the men are unionized."

"And where did you get all that from—one of Hawkins' speeches?"

"It's from the State Bureau of Mines," he said. "I telegraphed Mr. Robertson about it. He called it nonsense."

"He ought to know."

"But he staffed the Bureau."

She surprised him with a sob. Baxter hurried to her, but she slapped him away.

"What's going on?" he said.

"When are we leaving, Harlan? I'm going crazy out here all day long."

"You never mentioned anything before."

"It's a surprise to you? You're not that oblivious. You yourself came to me the other day and started talking about weapons, about how out of control things are."

"Didn't I ask you to leave? Didn't I do that?"

"I want us *all* to leave. What good would it do me to go back without a husband, for Thomas to go back without a father?"

"I can't leave until everything is put back in order."

"Those people are not your responsibility."

"Whose are they, then?"

She stormed from the kitchen. The front door slammed, but he didn't hear footsteps stomping off the porch. He allowed a minute or two to pass before going after her. She stood at the edge of the porch, arms crossed against the cold. Baxter submerged his hands in his robe, careful not to approach her when she wouldn't accept him.

"I love you," he said.

"For goodness sakes, Harlan. I love you, too. This has nothing to do with that."

Baxter rubbed her back with one hand. She did not resist his touch, nor did she soften toward him.

"The situation isn't clear-cut," he said.

"Nothing in life is," she said. "But don't expect me to care about my family less because of that." A breeze rolled through from the south and carried the sharp teeth of ice crystals. Lorraine shivered. Baxter coaxed her back into the house. She disappeared upstairs without kissing him.

In the kitchen, his water was boiling, but he had lost his appetite. He removed the pot from the heat, extinguished the burner with a little of the water. He poured himself more whiskey and sat in the parlor beside the window. A draft whipped across the floor and coiled around his ankles. He tucked a blanket over himself. Outside, the snow shined with smoothness. He closed his eyes, wondering what a person was supposed to do with a life.

Outside, the third-quarter moon climbed above the ridge. Only a few hours left. He knew he should be terrified. He was not. Boredom, then. Room for it in every situation, no matter how dire. Waiting in the tunnels, waiting for night, waiting for cover. They switched off their helmet lamps and told stories in the dark, voices disembodied by the blackness, beginning nowhere, ending nowhere. Garris talked, usually first, usually longest, somehow at ease.

"Eighty-six," he said. "You remember? Half a million of us out for the eight-hour day. Then Haymarket, which I wasn't nowhere near. Only read about it. Nobody knows who threw the bomb that killed them cops. Nobody knows how many dead in the end neither. Six cops for sure, and four wringed necks for the boys they blamed it on. For what? They'd read the wrong books."

Baxter did not remember. Too young. He also had only read about the riots that would have been visible from the old man's building. Shaw and his allies: "If the world must lose eight of its people, it can better afford to lose the eight members of the Illinois Supreme Court."

If I'd been old enough to witness it, to participate, would I have? He was ashamed because he knew the answer. He would have thought them nuisances, would have cheered the police who cleared them away. Before, history, dark friezes, scenarios performed by phantoms, connectionless. The past, dead tales told by doddering old men. No longer.

In the dark, in the tunnels, the past subsumed him. And it talked, became the present. Garris spoke. Baxter listened. He listened and Garris spoke and sometimes the others spoke in their own ways also.

"*Like I said, I wasn't nowhere near it. I was in Mississippi, working the cane. Down in Thibodaux. We threw in with the Knights of Labor. Went out, too. 'A dollar a day' we said. They were shafting us for seventy-five cents. Marched up and down those roads along the cane fields, ten thousand of us. Militia never far behind. We had 'em by the balls. Men don't work, ain't no product. No men in the fields, no sugar on the shelves. Listen to the Wobblies. Workers want to win? All they gotta do is fold their arms. The world comes to a stop. Ain't a continental thing happens without our hands to make it happen. Our hands in our pockets got more power than any Robertson. Shame, how few know it. They caught up with us in November. Rain fallin' like the sweat of the devil. Governor brought down martial law. We threatened the entire sugar crop, he said. Goddam right! That crop ain't nothin' but our sweat! They came after us. Took away Henry and George Cox. Never seen 'em again. Busted the Knights. We hit back, though. We had guns. We had blood. Shootin' all the time. They killed thirty of us, hundreds wounded. We got two of them. Torched what fields we could.*"

Baxter smelled the sickening sweet smoke of burning cane. He heard the shouts. Men fleeing, fighting.

"*I hid in the woods for a few days and hopped the first train north I could find. Chicago three days later. I was young then. Not no more. I'm old now. Feel old. Twenty-five years I spent in Chicago 'til I come here. Didn't much want to, but a man's gotta eat.*"

There were whispers, mumbles, feet shifting in the dirt.

17

Because it happened in the daytime, the arrival of the replacement workers was impossible to conceal. The train, pushing a bow wave of snow, entered the north end of the valley. A faint whistle grew into a shriek as the train neared the depot.

Lind established a perimeter around the depot, and, off to the side, another group of guards held the assembled strikers at bay. When Baxter walked by, the women spit on him. He wiped his face clean and tried to focus as he came abreast of Lind. "Are you set here?"

"Yes, sir." His horse was impatient. The brown snorting head tossed about until Lind yanked it back under control.

The train chuffed to a crawl, lurched, and stopped. Lind opened the cordon of horses into a semicircle and maneuvered against the boxcar doors. Baxter waited inside the cordon as the new workers detrained, shivering from the trip in the unheated boxcar. All of the new workers were black, their bodies draped with clothes even more ragged than the strikers'.

As the protective ring filled, the strikers grew restive. The whoosh and pummel of rifle butts on flesh punctuated unintelligible shouting. Then began a rain of snowballs and rocks. Baxter covered his head with his arms.

Lind, commanding and high in his stirrups, jerked the reins to and fro. His horse stomped out small, aggravated circles. The leather of Lind's saddle and leggings strained as he bellowed, "Hold your ground! The first load is almost out!"

When the last of the workers disembarked, the cordon closed into a circle again and moved off, pulsing but retaining its shape. A cloud of hate moved with it, cries from the strikers, a torrent of sound in foreign tongues, and angry responses in English. Baxter noticed a worker whose hair was flecked with gray and who appeared distraught over a private, unrelated matter. His overalls obscured a solid frame. Baxter guessed his age to be around fifty. The man shook his head and kicked at the ground, appearing to curse himself.

One of the guards teetered in his saddle when a rock hit him in the head. A ribbon of blood unfurled from his brow, yet he shook off the blow and leveled his rifle at a striker.

"No!" Baxter shouted as two shots rang out.

He fell to the ground, as did everyone around him. Cover, cover. Purest instinct. He pressed his face to the snow, thinking, That's it. That's the sound of the end. Then Lind ordered someone to back up.

Baxter did not hear footsteps.

Lind said, "Move back. You won't get another chance."

Baxter felt safe enough to look. Two puffs of smoke above Lind's pistol drifted to the west, the remains of his warning shots. The guard with the rifle had not fired. But now Lind had his pistol at a striker's head, and the man was still not moving.

"These are the last words you're ever going to hear," Lind said.

The man stepped away, and following him, the crowd receded. Lind holstered his pistol. The ringed workers stood up, Baxter with them, exhaling with relief, and they moved as a mass toward town. Baxter pushed himself from the circle of horses but stayed close by, walking with the group. As the crowd of strikers fractured and fell behind, he hoped that the company's shacks might be reoccupied without incident.

Hawkins yelled above the din. "Where's your solidarity, brothers? These strikers aren't your color, but they *are* your class! Stand with them! Stand with your brethren!"

"Hawkins!" Baxter called. One of the guards rode to Baxter's side. Baxter didn't send him away.

Rooted, Hawkins said, "I see two men, one of them mounted and armed, the other afoot and unarmed. And I dare say the second man appears allied with the first."

"I'm not going to joust with you today," Baxter said. He looked up at the guard. "Take Mr. Hawkins to jail, please."

"Now wait a minute," Hawkins attempted.

"No. We just saw a man come within a hair's breadth of being shot, and your first instinct was to provoke. I won't stand for it any longer. You are going back to jail."

"For how long?"

Baxter refused to answer. He crossed his arms, waiting.

Hawkins, scrutinizing him, said only, "Huh," clipped and calm. His hands were idle, his head angled in thought.

Baxter looked at the guard again. "Mr. Hawkins needs some motivation."

The guard's hand went for his club, but Hawkins said, "No need for that, friend. I'll go."

"Reach your hands up high," the guard said.

Hawkins obeyed. The guard threw a rope around his wrists, knotted it, and tied the other end to the pommel. The horse began a slow trot, and Hawkins had trouble keeping up. Each time he stumbled, the rope came taut and jerked him on.

Another horse galloped to Baxter and skidded to a stop. Lind dropped from a saddle. "Didn't think you had it in you."

"I've always had it in me," Baxter said. The crowd of strikers was dispersing quickly. "Tactics require forethought. What you interpret as weakness, as lack of resolve, is analysis. Our actions have to be judicious. You're too quick to attack."

"All I know is, it was about time you put that red bastard away."

~

The next week passed in uneasy calm. The new workers fell straight into the hillside shacks and then into work. The strikers returned to camp, apparently to wait for Hawkins' release. Let them wait, Baxter thought. He took it upon himself to ensure satisfactory food and treatment for Hawkins, but the stasis his imprisonment precipitated did not bode well for his freedom. Baxter thought it might be best to keep him locked up indefinitely, as the strikers appeared rudderless without him. Meanwhile, production recovered. Tonnage approached half of pre-strike levels. Mr. Robertson might choose to keep the new workers forever. A quiescent operation running at half capacity could be preferable to a volatile one generating twice the output. The realization sent Baxter up to the shacks.

On the trail, two more inches of recent snow had been packed down by foot traffic. Baxter slipped as he ascended the bluff. When his feet strayed just off the path, undisturbed snow rose up in powdery clouds.

Lind had posted a guard before every block of shacks to protect against reprisals from the strikers. Baxter walked to each dwelling in search of the man who'd caught his attention at the depot. He didn't know why he was seeking this one man in particular. Perhaps the draw was the gray-flecked hair, a possible sign of an older man's cooler temperament.

He reached the last of the shacks, about fifteen strung along the hillside on the highest row. Finally the correct door opened. A lean man with broad shoulders. He had the drooping posture that age brings to men who pass through younger, bulkier days. His neck was distinctive, pillared with weathered muscle. "Yeah?"

"I want to talk to you about the situation here."

He looked at Baxter for a long time before retreating into the shack, leaving the door open behind him as a resigned invitation. He took a seat at a small table where a younger man waited, thinner, more wiry, and with thicker hair. A checkerboard lay in progress.

Baxter entered and looked around for somewhere to sit. He saw no chairs other than the two at the table. A mattress frame and blankets occupied one corner, but Baxter was not going to sit on another man's bed without first being asked. "I want to tell you what's been happening lately."

The older man scoffed. "We know all about it." From his pocket, he extracted a slip of paper and handed it to Baxter.

NIGERRS GIT OWT NOW OR WE BLO YOO OWT.

The scrawl was halting and childish, a threat written by a semi-literate.

"How did this get to you?" Baxter asked.

"Came under the door. Saw it after we woke. What good are guards when this shit gets through? You the damn security chief round here, ain't you?"

"No, I'm not. I'll say that much for myself. My name is Harlan Baxter." He extended his hand, which the older man eyed and left untouched.

"Name's Willie Garris. This here's Al Pierce."

Pierce, who looked about ten years younger than Garris, shook Baxter's hand. "We come on out from Chicago."

"I hope the trip was satisfactory." He winced at how stupid he sounded.

Garris said, "Top-shelf. We felt like regular prize cattle. Now, are you gonna say something useful, 'cause if not, we got a game to finish."

"I'm trying to calm things down," Baxter said. "I'm trying to resolve the whole dispute here."

"Try harder," Garris said.

Baxter did not retort. He could not find his footing. Garris leaned back in his chair, crossed his arms with satisfaction.

"What you offer 'em so far?" Pierce asked.

"A hike in tonnage rates and a flat fee for dead work."

"How much?"

"All told, a few dollars more per week."

"That ain't an offer," Garris said. "That's shit. That's nigger wages."

Pierce kicked him under the table. Garris said, "What are you worried about? He just got us here. He ain't gonna send us out for a little sass. Ain't that right, Baxter?"

"Yes."

"And they askin' for what?" Pierce said.

"More money. Unionization."

"And you ain't gonna give it up to 'em, huh?" Garris said.

"The union? Mr. Robertson wouldn't hear of it."

"I don't see a Mr. Robertson here. I see you."

"It's not my decision."

"Say it was."

"It doesn't matter. I don't have the power to affect that issue, so why speculate?"

"Don't matter? What power those folks in those tents got? None, but it sure matters to them. I figure it ought to matter to you, 'specially since its your ass if you don't sort 'em out. Ain't that right again?"

"In a manner of speaking."

"You got yourself a problem."

"Do you have any advice?"

Garris laughed. "Sure. Fuck you. Fuck the company. You ain't doing us no favors. You white folks go on keep up with your war. Next day me and Al'll still have to scrape by as usual."

Pierce said, "Sorry 'bout him, Mr. Baxter."

"That's all right," Baxter said. Remarkable how thick the skin grows when the alternative is bullets, he thought. "Keep in mind, the company won't wait forever for the strikers to come to their senses. In time, Mr. Robertson will choose an entirely new workforce. You fellows have been doing a fine job, all of you. Maybe a place could be made here for you permanently."

Garris kept his eyes on the checker board. "You hear that, Al? They gonna turn this here mine into a nigger mine. Robertson's got the reform spirit and boss man's 'bout to bring down salvation."

Pierce said to Baxter, "You serious?"

"'Course he ain't," Garris said.

"You hush." Again to Baxter, Pierce said, "You're talking good jobs here?"

"There's an excellent chance of that. Maybe soon I can say more."

Pierce deflated.

"I told you he was shoveling," Garris said. "Tell you what, Baxter. You leave us be while we dig coal for you. If we quit doin' that, then come on back. Meantime, the air around here is hard enough to breathe without your smoke, too."

Baxter left in impotence, the bungling of the visit weighing on him. On his way home, his mind turned over and over. Even if the union was not as poor as Hawkins indicated, strike funds weren't unlimited. Feeding and housing so many people so far from a major city had to be prohibitively expensive, especially considering the distribution costs. Certainly the financing the union could bring to bear on the situation was infinitesimal compared to the company's resources. From the union's perspective, the current state of affairs couldn't persist much longer. Add to it the note Garris had showed him. Startling. Behaving like a bunch of hoodlums wouldn't help the strikers' cause. Nevertheless, what they'd endured in the camp, let alone in the mines, had proven their stamina, and they showed no signs of giving in. On both sides, lives were at risk that did not need to be.

The time had come for everyone to moderate their demands. He had to choose who sacrificed first. The strikers had so far shown more restraint than Lind had. Therefore, as a sign of goodwill, Baxter decided to send half the guards home. He could not see a way forward while the valley still brimmed with them. Afterward, if the strikers matched his concession, he would order some of the scabs from the coalfields. In this way, incremental steps toward normalcy could be achieved.

Dispatching the guards, however, would not be easy. The old man hovered as a mercurial specter, which was why Baxter had stopped informing him about arguably minor events. But now, upon the loss of half of his workforce, Lind would certainly want to know if such a drastic change in policy had been approved from the top.

Thus, Baxter prepared himself to lie. In the morning he would claim he'd already cleared the withdrawal order with Mr. Robertson. With luck, the guards would be back in Denver and scattered through the city before anyone was the wiser. Simultaneously, the strikers would have to drop their demand for unionization and accept Baxter's plan for de-escalation. Failing that, he would threaten permanent replacement of the workforce. If the ruses worked long enough for him to get the mine running at capacity again, he might avoid all second-guessing. In fact, he might be commended for his foresight.

They worked together, wrapping charges, laying them aside, wrapping more. Piles of them grew, some with fuses, others with contacts for wire detonation. They laid the materials into separate piles, their hands working as automatons, repetition having taught them the motions.

The older men held sway. Baxter understood. Fifty. Garris' age. As far as Baxter could tell, Garris was the most senior among them. Not old by normal standards, ancient for a miner. Alive and uninjured at fifty hinted at indestructibility.

"Tell you about Pullman," Garris said, his hands working with smooth deliberation. "1894. I followed that one in the papers."

Baxter said, "I read about it in school, years later." Robertson's role made him sick now to remember. The mammoth factory designed for a railroad stranglehold, one factory big enough to control the whole industry, among the first to use assembly lines, not for efficiency but to break craft unions.

Garris said, "Pierce and me would'a been unskilled trash there, too. Niggers at the bottom there, too. Company town with houses and gardens."

"Like those on the bluff?" Baxter said.

"Nothing like them. Pullman built a bosses' headquarters, high as a cathedral, big spike at the top. Lake Vista out front and shops to all sides."

Baxter recalled some images. The central promenade thronged at noontime. Among the first photos ever in a newspaper.

"Then, 1893," Garris said.

"My family was wiped out," Baxter said.

"How'd it feel to hit bottom?" Pierce asked.

"We staggered along."

"Not much of a dance, huh?"

"Pullman slashed the wages," Garris said. "The workers didn't want to strike at first, but Pullman wouldn't talk, wouldn't say nothin' to them. Take it or leave it. They left it."

Pierce said, "Debs."

The single syllable triggered murmurs of respect, each man contributing. They all knew at least that one name.

Garris said, "Debs calls the strike and men stream out like Joshua is blowing for them. They line up before the main gate and shut the whole works down. For a while it looked like they'd win. The Chicago stories were pretty evenhanded. Pullman had made his enemies. Then the torches came out, and, well, you could just as well call it war."

"Bastards put mail cars on the trains before Debs and his boys blocked them," Pierce said.

"Federal offense," Baxter said.

"Troops," Garris said.

18

Baxter sat down in a chair before the cell.

"Yes, I'm being treated fairly," Hawkins said. "Yes, I'm being fed regularly, and, yes, I'm being allowed to sleep. How many times are you going to ask me the same questions? I'll stipulate that you're a humane jailer so we can progress to other issues."

"I can leave now if you'd like."

"And go where—back to your wife? I'm surprised she's still talking to you after you dragged her to Colorado and cooped her up."

Without a word, Baxter moved toward the exit.

"Wait," Hawkins said, an unmistakable hint of nervousness in his voice. "That was rude of me. I'm sorry."

Baxter stopped.

"Please, come back and we'll talk. My temper is a little short these days. Boredom."

Against his better judgment, Baxter sat down again.

Cautiously, Hawkins said, "You can't keep me in here forever."

"I can keep you here as long as I please."

Hawkins tapped the bars of the cell. "Better than a tent in some ways. At least I know you're not going to flatten it."

"I don't agree with everything the company does."

"And yet it does it all the same."

"I promise that if you call off the strike I'll lean on the old man for more concessions. I'll have more sway once I'm back in New York.

I can't persuade him of anything over a telegraph wire. There's no humanness to it. No feel. I'll plead your case directly to him, right to his face. I promise to go to bat for the men. Don't you believe me?"

"I do."

"So, take the offer. Please."

"It's not up to me. And anyway, I couldn't do it."

"Why not?"

"Because we shouldn't even be negotiating with you."

"And why is that?"

"We don't recognize you as a legitimate advocate, just as we don't recognize the company as a legitimate entity. We don't concede that a company should be treated as a person. Valid contracts must be negotiated between people of reasonably matched power. But between people and a company? Between people and an artificial construct, a legal fiction? I'm sorry. A man might as well negotiate with a punctuation mark. Still, the world has its current workings. We must accommodate them from time to time."

"I am a man. Mr. Robertson is a man."

"You, yes. Robertson, no. He's too rich to be a man anymore. With enough money, a man turns into his money. His humanity becomes just the wallet he carries it in." Hawkins shifted as if with insight. "You don't like me very much, do you?"

"My personal feelings aren't at issue."

"Maybe not, but I'd still like to know. Don't worry, I won't be offended."

"You're not my favorite person, no."

"Why is that? I should think you'd warm to someone of your own type. I'm more like you than anyone else in this valley, and yet you side with Lind."

"I look at you, and I don't see a man. I see a machine. A machine spewing rhetoric and ideas."

"Do they motivate?"

"I just insulted you. Do me the service of not enjoying it."

"I ask you again, my ideas, do they motivate?"

"They do, yes, in a sense, but it's the motivation of an avalanche."

"One of the highest compliments I've ever received!"

"Which means it's blind, chaotic, destructive. It builds nothing but a stampede."

"The imagery of the herd? Come now, Baxter, you can try harder than that. 'If every Athenian citizen had been a Socrates, every Athenian assembly would still have been a mob.' Who said it?"

"Without you, the men in that camp would listen to reason."

"One man's reason is another man's madness, Baxter. But don't dodge the question. Who said it?"

"Napoleon."

"Incorrect. Our own James Madison."

"Which proves what?"

"That ours is a long-running struggle. It's not something we chose. It was forced upon us from the first days of the republic when the founders decided that collective action by the people should be thwarted."

"We are not participating in the grand unfolding of history. We are in the middle of a wage dispute, nothing more. There's nothing so grandiose about it. I believe I can get the men more money eventually, but a few cents now are not worth all this trouble."

"That's right," Hawkins said. "Therefore all this trouble can't be over a few cents."

"You just won't give an inch, will you?"

"I don't see that I have to."

"You're manipulative. You're pushing those strikers where they wouldn't otherwise go."

"This time it's you who's being careless with history. This strike started before I got here."

"They knew they had your support, or the union's support, I mean."

"You're wrong about that. In fact, I'll let you in on a secret. When the strike request came to the union, I was on the committee for authorization."

"I thought you were just an organizer."

"I have official capacities, too. We're shorthanded, as are most organizations like ours, so we have to double our efforts. In any case, don't you want to know how I voted?"

"I already know that. The strike is on."

"Yes, but it was a committee decision, with yours truly dissenting, quite vigorously, as it happened."

"Why was it authorized?"

"I was outvoted. The majesty of democracy. Truth be told, I see the situation basically as you do. Robertson is a brick wall, and a strike here just drains resources we could use to greater effect elsewhere. Frankly, I was shocked you pushed for *any* concessions."

"Call it off, then," Baxter implored. "Call it off before people get hurt."

"People are already hurting. And they've rallied around my cause, not yours. Anyway, you could recognize the union and solve everything at a stroke."

"You know that's impossible. You said it yourself."

"True, but I'm only authorized to declare victory. The strikers themselves have to concede defeat."

"That's absurd. You see things more clearly than they do."

"Even if that were true, it's irrelevant. I follow their orders, not the other way around."

Baxter stood and turned his back on the cell.

"I could very easily go back to New York or Chicago or wherever and live a different life," Hawkins continued. "A much easier one. The stock markets and corporations are waiting for me. I have the pedigree. I could just as well choose a life outside the movement as inside."

"Why don't you, then?"

Hawkins looked him over for a long moment. "What do you know about Shays' Rebellion?"

"Can't you give me a straight answer for once in your life? I don't need another history lesson."

"You don't have to listen. Last time I checked, I'm the captive audience, not you."

Frustrated, Baxter said, "Shays' Rebellion was a tax revolt in Massachusetts."

"Much more than that. Poor farmers were losing their land to the bankers, and they took up arms for debt-relief . . ."

Only half listening, Baxter wandered away from the cell. Hawkins was more relentless jailed than free. Imprisoned and isolated for days, his reservoir of words must have been rising all the while. Conversation opened the sluices. He might flow for hours now. Baxter could think of little to say to someone so intoxicated with the sound of his own voice, so lacking in skepticism about rhetoric. The world is made of people, not words. Hawkins either did not see this, or he saw it and ignored it. Yet I linger around him, Baxter thought. Why?

". . . as veterans of the Revolution, Baxter, they were motivated by the idea that since independence had been won by the efforts of all, the property of the United States should be the property of all . . ."

He is in motion, Baxter thought, passionate motion. That simplicity could be the explanation for his draw. One encounters so seldom a personality which presses with any force, but Hawkins assaults with his shoulders lowered. His voice was cleansed of insincere syllables, which had nothing to do with being right, but rather with the ability to command attention, to be reckoned with. Moreover, Hawkins was clearly having fun, and there was something frightening about that. His joy disguised a malice inherent in his personality which, uncontrolled, was unpredictable. Of what value was someone so obscured by his own verbal mist, visible yet shapeless and failing to come into focus?

". . . and that's why the Constitution so restricts democracy. Shays' Rebellion was the specter that chilled James Madison to his bones. Nowadays we toss around words like democracy, freedom, rights, and so on, but they mean nothing divorced from people's willingness to put their lives on the line to defend them. That's what Madison meant when he said that a parchment barrier would never be a protection for freedom. About *that* at least he has my total agreement."

Silence. Miraculous silence.

"Are you through?" Baxter asked.

"I'm just trying to place our struggle in its proper context."

"You left out the most important thing."

"What's that?"

"They lost," Baxter said. "Shays and his boys. They lost. They were hunted down and killed. Let us clear away the fog." He stabbed at Hawkins with his finger. "You will lose this strike, Mr. Hawkins, and the people in those tents will lose right along with you. You're toying with them, and you don't respect them enough to tell them the truth."

"False. Mr. Chamm and I have discussed these issues extensively. The strikers have relented too many times before, and this time, they want to persevere. As human beings, they're free to follow whomever they choose, whatever ideas they choose, take whatever actions they choose."

"Even into ruin?"

"Or into salvation. Or beyond either. They will create their own futures. They can do nothing with the brittle reality they face now. They have to shatter it. Haven't you ever wanted to smash something just because it offends the human spirit? Think of the abolitionists, Baxter. They didn't negotiate with slavery. They attacked and attacked until they made it burn. Plenty of them died before new life sprung from its ashes. But by your logic, their fight was in vain because they did not live to see success."

"It's not the same thing."

Hawkins smirked at him.

"It's *not*," Baxter said. "What's going on in this valley is not good, but it's not slavery."

"Fair enough, sir, fair enough. Nevertheless, what would you have me say to my people after all that's happened? That despite all the promises the company has broken in the past, this time will be different because Harlan Baxter has spoken? They wouldn't believe me, and they shouldn't."

"Then we are at an impasse."

"For the moment."

"That's unacceptable."

"You have my pity, Baxter. Life for you must be a tremendous trial. You eat, then you're hungry again. You sleep, then you're tired again. This is a burden to you when it should be a joy, a path to happiness and freedom. Fulfillment lies in the pursuit of the unattainable, yes? The artists are never satisfied. The revolutionaries are never satisfied. Nor the saints, nor the philosophers."

"They are miserable. The great ones especially."

"But they are fully human. They throw themselves into the human project. And don't forget how many of them have been the offspring of the ruling classes. Leisure was theirs for the taking. Couldn't they have chosen lives of repose, of comfort? Certainly they could have. They didn't want to because they understood the essential fact that you, too, as an intelligent man, understand. The difference is that they accepted it whereas you resist it."

"This fact being?"

"That in the end we lie in the ground forever. Emerging from oblivion, we return thereto, and much too rapidly."

Baxter tugged at his own hair. "Life is not pointless."

"Who said it was?"

"You did just then!"

"Because I don't believe in an afterlife?" Hawkins laughed. "What has that got to do with it?"

"Don't laugh at me. I don't deserve it. I've treated you with respect."

"You have, but I'm sorry. I can't help it. We're all going to die, Baxter. Should we therefore die after a brutal and servile life? Shouldn't we spend it squeezing what life we can from it, helping others to do the same? No more sentimentality. We must learn to value struggle or we are lost."

Baxter crumpled Garris' note and threw it through the bars. "Here's your Fellowship of Man."

Hawkins read the note, shaking his head. "It's a shame. We can be petty creatures. Short memories, limited imaginations. It's hard for some men to see beyond their prejudices. This kind of thing is so counterproductive. Listen to Debs, though. You don't hear any of this bigoted claptrap from him."

"Debs isn't here."

Hawkins returned the note and sat down again, slumped this time and for once quiet. He folded his hands, and, with his eyes half closed, he bowed his head. Had Baxter not known better, he would have sworn he was praying.

"Mr. Hawkins, please look at me."

Hawkins obliged him.

"Right now, mankind is you, me, and the people in that camp. Eugene Victor Debs does not appear in the census. But with or without him, you will lose this strike."

"Probably, but the outcome depends on what people do, and we can never predict that. Any assumption about what's going to happen in the future is absurd."

"Please, listen," Baxter implored.

"We do what we think is right."

"And when you're about to fail, what do you do then?"

Hawkins shrugged. "Hold fast. *Fiat justitia ruat caelum.*"

Baxter felt sluggish, as if Hawkins had shorted out vital wires within him, and after all their back and forth, all his thinking, the available options had not changed. Baxter closed his eyes, weighing for a last time his decision, barely believing he was about to follow through on it. "It's hard enough to keep Lind and the strikers apart. Can you keep your people off the scabs?"

"Not from in here."

"And if I release you?"

Guardedly, Hawkins said, "I'm entitled to my freedom as a matter of justice, not as a matter of pragmatism."

"You're not entitled to anything. Just tell me whether you could control your people."

"I'd do my best."

"You could keep them in line?"

"I think so. As long as I have anything to do with it, we won't start a fight."

Baxter unlocked the cell.

Hawkins came out. He watched the door swing back until it latched. Only then did he turn his attention to Baxter. "Thank you."

"Tomorrow I'm ordering half of those Pinkertons back to Denver."

"More good news. Can I ask why?"

"I'm convinced they're adding to the troubles, not preventing them."

"I agree."

"Don't mistake this for weakness. The company still has plenty of men available. There will be strength enough to put you down if necessary."

"Understood." Looseness returned to Hawkins' limbs as he realized that he was indeed released. "What about you, Baxter? Do you believe me?"

Baxter lifted his coat from the desk. "As far as I can tell, you haven't lied to me yet. If you say you'll try to keep your men under control, I don't have much choice but to believe you."

"Then it appears the future has unexpectedly brought me my freedom."

"Harlan Baxter brought you your freedom. Put it to good use."

"Thank you for proving my point anyway."

Dear God, enough, Baxter thought as he left.

~

In the morning, Baxter called Lind to the office and showed him the release order for Hawkins along with the withdrawal memo for the Pinkertons. Baxter sat placidly behind the desk.

"You can't be serious," Lind said, setting the papers down.

Baxter wanted to avoid debate, so he sighed and blinked slowly for effect, no anger conveyed, just the exasperation he might employ with Thomas to correct a moment of stubbornness. Baxter took up the papers, opened a drawer of the filing cabinet, and leafed through it. "I assure you I am. I'll even arrange bonuses if you like."

"Mr. Baxter, it's the wrong move."

Baxter slammed the drawer. "I am not going to have this discussion again. Ludlow is *my* mine."

"I'm asking you to reconsider."

"I've analyzed it to distraction. The last thing this town needs right now is a battery of agitated gun thugs. They're going back to Denver. I've already cleared it with Mr. Robertson. Follow my orders or I'll have your job." Steadfast, Baxter watched the coils tighten within Lind, while outside, the usual noise of the town mutated into what sounded like a fight. Lind looked out the window and immediately left the office.

Baxter hurried after him. The street was filled with people. The strikers had turned out for another march, blocking passage for the changing shifts. Guards, some mounted, some afoot, had formed a wall of protection. Hawkins stood at the front of the strikers, and at the sight of him, Baxter was apoplectic. Somehow he swallowed the desperate, unintelligible sound that was tearing to escape his lungs. Somehow he kept his hands from seizing Hawkins.

"There are strikers in the street," Baxter sputtered. "Someone promised me this would not happen again."

"I pleaded with them not to do it," Hawkins said. His face was pained with worry and sympathy and unquestionable regret. "I begged them, but they went ahead anyway."

"Disavow them!"

"I can't do that," Hawkins said. "I want to help you. I owe you that. But I can't. They've made their choice. I have to support them."

Lind pushed Baxter aside and stood face-on with Hawkins. "Move," Lind said.

"No," Hawkins said.

Lind drew his pistol and fired twice into Hawkins' chest.

Blind men working, scratching. What they assembled could be called talking, could be called speech. Baxter cleaved to Garris, drawn by the ease of communication, experience. The length of his life. He and Pierce had smashed against the Wobblies, had joined the beef strikes that Sinclair covered. Two in the sixty thousand that walked, a strike regarded as lunacy. A million and a half men were roaming the country, looking for work, a hundred thousand of them in Chicago alone. Scabs galore, the packers eager to hire. Still the men walked.

Garris said, "A man ain't a dog, and six dollars a week is a dog's wage. A whole life of dog's wages ain't gonna get you a shack to piss in or an alley to sing the blues. People talk about Sinclair, the big hero. Read what he says about us. Calls us criminals and thugs. Big black bucks stealin' the utensils and such, grindin 'em to a point to carry in our boots. Said our wooly heads only come 'round for the white women. Says we come for disorder, not wages. We come for work! Scabs, sure, but what union wants us? You go ahead and read him. Might as well say, 'Nigger go home.' Fuck Sinclair. He never done nothin' for us."

The noise of Garris' hands died out. He spoke with diminished heat. "Pierce says I'm mad at everything. He don't see it my way. Way he sees it, Sinclair did right by us. Says Sinclair did about all you can expect a cracker to do."

Garris scraped at the dirt, breathing harder. "Been fightin' Sinclairs my whole life. You in here with us is better than all the Sinclairs out there with them. I don't even care why you're here. Workers is workers, what I say. But that's something everybody got to lead hisself to."

Pack the charge. Wrap it. Install contacts. Install a fuse. Again. Listen. Watch. Think.

Stories, some complete, others, mere shards, jagged pieces of English, Polish, and Italian blasted from whole tongues, curses, too, drawings in the dirt, wild gesticulations and careful, quiet pantomime.

Santino made himself rigid with mock formality, grasping imaginary lapels. In the dust, outlines of Italy and America. "Di dove sei, giovanotto?" he said, answering himself in a meeker voice. "Dalla campagna." He drew a barn and two stick-figure animals.

A farm, Baxter thought. He scrambled for his elementary Latin. Pointing at Santino, he said, "Agricola?"

"Si! Si! Agricoltore!"

"He's a farmer," Baxter said.

"Was one," Garris said.

Again in his solemn pose, Santino spoke. "In America guadagnerai abbastanza in una settimana per comprare tre fattorie." He drew arrows from Italy to America, dollar signs around the latter. He drew a ship in the space between the continents, then doled out imaginary dollar bills. "Non ti piacerebbe un viaggio gratuito per l'America?"

"He was recruited, I think," Baxter said. "He's imitating the recruiter." Santino circled the ship and put hash marks beside it. A scrape of his hand shoved the marks into the hull. He pushed more and more marks aboard.

"Transatlantic, maybe," Baxter said. "Steerage."

"Come schiavi," Santino said. He pointed emphatically at Garris. "Come schiavi!"

"Packed you in, did they?" Garris said. "Well, not so bad as we had it, but anyway slave color don't matter. Only matters you poor. Maybe you learned it too late, but you learned it."

One of the Poles took up the recruiter's stance. Gestures of buying drinks, laying out contracts from within briefcases. "Mogę ci kupić piwo?" The Pole took a drink. "Jeszcze jedno?" Feigned another and another. Staggering, he said, "Wkrótce byłem pijany." He smoothed out a rectangle of dust, drew a line at its bottom for a signature. "Chesz dostać pracę? Proszę podpisać umowę tutaj." He signed. His hand swept over the contract. "Nie potrafię czytać, ale byłem zbyt pijany żeby się tym przejmować."

Easy to guess what happened next. Cattle cars and drink. Trains to West Virginia. Kentucky. Pennsylvania.

Colorado.

"Z Polski do Ameryki." The Pole gestured at himself dismissively. "Nic się nie zmieniło." Look at me, said his hands. Look at what I've made of myself. Look at where life has delivered me.

Wrap it. Contacts. Fuse.

Garris again. "We seen the lay of it after Chicago. Saw a flyer for workers to come here. Pierce even asked as we gettin' on the train, 'There any union where we goin? Cuz I don't want no union skimming my wages,' all sly like. What he want more than a union? What we want more than that? A real union, one that'll take in ALL men, white and black, and treat 'em like men. A union like Debs wants, 'cept they won't let him have it. Anyway we don't say nothin' about Debs. The boss man says, 'Don't worry about it. It's a new mine. Ain't even been worked yet.'"

Baxter listened, made his charges. Darkness but for the parade of images.

"So we got on the train. Didn't believe the man exactly. We been around. We know how the man do whenever he do it, but we too poor to fuss about it. A whole stinkin' life spent grabblen around in the dirt and nothin' to show for it but a dry gut-rumble. Gotta take a chance. We shiver our asses halfway across this country. They dump us out into a riot, and all the time I'm kickin' myself for foolishness. And that first night Pierce and I talked. Pierce said that we get a chance, don't you know we'd better take it. Tired of this bullshit travelin' all the time, foldin' up our lives every time white folks too crazy to see who can help 'em and who can't. He said, 'If this camp cracks open, we oughtta pry. We oughtta turn those cracks into canyons.' He was right with it, right with it all the way. Said, 'Bunch a fired-up niggers in a coalpile ain't somethin' they banked on. Stand back and watch. It'll be the night runnin' wild. Ain't near enough pattyrollers in this valley to do a thing about it. We'll come on like Colonel Holloway gettin' his ashes hauled.'"

"I didn't know, not until he was next to me."

"He covered it up 'round folks who didn't need to see."

"I didn't protect him."

"You want shame, you carry it if you want to. Fact is, there's no way to go he would've liked better."

Wrap. Contact. Fuse. Again.

19

Hawkins fell and scuttled backward on the ground. His face twisted as the two small holes in his chest gave up freshets of blood. He passed his hand gingerly across the wounds as if he'd discovered his shirt to be inexplicably missing two buttons. In seconds, his jaw fell slack, his eyes mute.

Lind offered Baxter the gun. "Run your mine, Mr. Baxter."

Baxter could not think. He said only, "Why did you do that?"

The air exploded with rage as the strikers roared forward. Lind seized Baxter's shirt and hauled him behind the mounted guards as the foot soldiers charged. Men crashed together, thumping, slashing, merging like slides of rock, pounding without mercy at each other. Baxter did not hear more shots as the street became a whirl of milling legs, billy clubs rising and falling, desperate punches. Here, a striker plunged his finger two-knuckles deep into a guard's eye. There, a guard worked methodically with a club, smashing first the knee, then the kidney, then the head as he struck and struck amid splashing blood. Elsewhere, a striker landed a crossing blow and a fallen guard got his stomach stomped. Ribs broke with revolting, audible snaps. Everywhere beneath the shouts and curses thudded an awful, continuous substrate of blows. From time to time a striker threw himself toward the line of horses. The mounted guards, advantaged of height and leverage, swept low and hard with rifle butts and clubs, knocking strikers down. The horseline fell back in unison, keeping the scabs protected and slowing the advance of strikers by forcing them to step over their fallen predecessors.

Again Lind shoved the pistol on Baxter. "Are you going to run this operation or not?"

"You just killed a man!"

"Self-defense."

Chamm tumbled, one eye bloody, from the maelstrom. He spun and stumbled, fell, picked himself up, ran toward Baxter and Lind, his feet skidding on the snow, frictionless. Lind aimed the pistol. Baxter smashed down on his arm. The weapon dropped from Lind's grasp. Lind's fist made heavy contact with Baxter's skull. Baxter reeled without losing consciousness. By the time his twirling senses found purchase again, Lind and Chamm had fallen on each other, biting, clawing, ripping in the snow. Lind worked close with jabs until Chamm caught his wrist and twisted it. Lind howled, and they rolled again, this time to Chamm's advantage, and he swept pendulum blows to Lind's head. Lind kicked him away. Chamm wasn't able to recover. Lind pounced on his chest and slammed his head, again and again, into the ground. Baxter ordered, "Stop!" but Lind persisted, so Baxter tackled him. Lind rolled away and came up again with a short burst of manic laughter. He didn't counterattack, and the sound of his laughter, the clarity of it in the air, made Baxter realize the fighting had stopped. The mounted guards remained in formation, but no more miners charged. The street was paved with groaning bodies that soon began to stand and separate, helping others of their kind back behind their respective lines.

Chamm, heaving on all fours, pushed himself up to his knees. Wavering, with red welts across his face and bleeding from the cheek, he said, "Straight murder now? That's the new rules?"

Lind spat a crimson mist. He wiped his mouth. "Same rules as always." He spoke, hobbled by panting, to all. "Understood? Same

rules as always! Niggers work! As long as wops, hunkies, and shee-
nies don't work, niggers work! That's the way it is, that's the way it's
gonna be! Hawkins got what strikers get when they disobey orders.
Learn from him so I don't have to teach you later." He steadied himself, fists repositioned, and said to Chamm, "What about you? You
ready for more?"

Chamm struggled to his feet. Haltingly, he joined the other strikers
as they slouched toward camp. Lind whistled after them, kicking at
Hawkins' body, the blood-soaked snow a red cape beneath it. "Don't
forget to pick up your garbage." Two strikers dragged the body away,
painting a long smear of blood across the street. Lind signaled for the
guards to escort the scabs to the mines. As he passed, Garris caught
Baxter's gaze and held it, the former's face blank, placid, inscrutable.

"*That's* the way you run a mine, Baxter," Lind said.

Baxter trembled with shock and adrenaline. "F-f-fired."

"Me? Uh huh." Lind handed him a crumpled telegram.

> I SYMPATHIZE WITH DIFFICULTIES STOP PRODUCTION
> PARAMOUNT STOP OVERRIDE BAXTER IF NECESSARY STOP
> P.D.R.

"You ain't the only man can use a wire," Lind said. "Go home and
get your wife and kid out of that house before we have to come and
throw you out. Strikers can't stay in company housing."

~

Chamm held a piece of burlap filled with snow against his swollen
face. He waved in Baxter and his bedraggled family. In the tent, a
lantern glowed weakly. Anna and Oliver sat near the stove.

"Don't take no disgrace at comin' here," Anna said. "Company
wickedness brought this on you." She filled a pot with water and

placed it on the stove. For Lorraine, Chamm opened the trap and pulled up another chair from beneath the floor.

Baxter could not bring himself to sit. Every nerve in his body was firing in unison. His head throbbed from Lind's punch. He felt ready to burst apart, but the tent was far too small for him to pace. He could only stand and fidget.

Chamm gave him another piece of burlap. "Make yourself a pack. Something on you gotta hurt bad enough to need it." Baxter wrapped some snow into the cloth and pressed it to his head where Lind's blow had landed. The cold was shocking but effective.

When the water on the stove boiled, Anna poured in a cupful of lentils and a bit of salt. At the scent of food, Baxter realized he was ravenously hungry. Chamm offered cigarettes. Lorraine took one. Chamm lit hers and his own. They both inhaled. Baxter watched his wife with surprise.

"I used to sneak them from my father, but I quit before I met you." Her hands were shaking, her face ashen.

After the riot, Baxter had torn into the house. "Get a bag," he'd said to Lorraine. "Stuff whatever you can into it. We can't stay here."

"I thought I heard shots not long ago. Please tell me I didn't hear shots."

"Where's Thomas?"

"Upstairs. Harlan, what's going on?"

"Thomas! Down here now!"

The boy came down holding a sheet of paper covered with sums. "I finished early today. Can we play checkers later?"

"I don't know, son. We'll see. First you need to start gathering your clothes, not everything, just enough for a couple of days. Your mother and I will be up soon to help. Go, go, go."

He pushed the boy along and began his own frantic scavenging of the house, choosing supplies. A coat, a hat, boots. "Don't dally," he said to Lorraine. "Help me."

"Tell me what's happening."

"Hawkins is dead."

"What? How?"

"Lind shot him."

"Was it an accident?"

The question stopped him. "Lind shot him for no reason. No reason at all."

"Harlan, you're frightening me. Tell me what happened. You're not telling me anything."

Baxter tried to swallow. His throat wouldn't allow it. "The strikers blocked a shift. There was a confrontation. I can't explain it all to you now. We need to pack. We'll take the first train out tomorrow morning."

"Where's Lind?"

"Where do you think? He's supervising the shift."

"The mine is still running? Harlan, shut it down! Lind needs to be arrested!"

Baxter was shaking with upheaval. "And who's going to arrest him? He's the chief of security."

"Fire him."

Baxter coughed out a bitter laugh. "I tried that. The old man cut me off at the knees. I saw the telegram. I couldn't believe it."

"Whatever he said, it can't apply to murder. You have to tell him."

"What good would that do? He gave Lind the power to overrule me. Anyway, Lind wouldn't let me near the telegraph now. It's out of my hands. Mr. Robertson will have to contact Governor Ammons. It's a state issue." He shook off the conversation. "None of this matters now. Just pack. Please."

He could think of only one haven, and now they'd reached it unharmed. Anna's wooden spoon clunked dully on the side of the pot. He felt overwhelmed with gratitude. One night's safe harbor put him in Chamm's debt forever. He sat down and had to lean forward to keep his collar dry of the dripping of the ice pack.

Anna looked into the soup and frowned. "Toss another shovel of coal in," she said. "Stove's gone cool."

Chamm rose and opened the door to the stove, plunging a small scoop into a box of coal scraps. He shoveled the fuel in, and a tongue of unobstructed heat licked Baxter's shins. Chamm evened out the burn with a long piece of iron. The coals, exposed to the air, glowed more vigorously and rose into flame. Baxter was momentarily hypnotized as the fire moved and fluctuated.

"Smart to get out of there quick," Chamm said as he closed the stove. "If Lind had come after you, I figure he would have killed you."

Anna glared at her husband. "Why'd you have to say that?"

"I didn't say nothin'," Chamm said, but his eyes dropped to the floor.

Lorraine began to cry openly, unable to help herself, and Thomas joined her. Anna went to them. "Here now, shush," she said. "You all give me a hand with dinner and calm down." She drew them to the stove before turning on the men. "You two git on outta here for a while."

"It's cold!" Chamm protested.

Anna pointed her spoon at him. "Don't care," she said. "Folks come in here all wound up, and you go shootin' your mouth off."

Chamm grumbled incoherently as he threw on his coat.

"Men could screw up a free lunch," Anna said.

Into the frigid night, Baxter followed Chamm a short distance down one walkway. Then Chamm stopped and chose another route. Baxter wanted to return to his family—he'd not wanted to leave them in the first place—but Anna had the run of her own tent, and Baxter wasn't in a position to contradict her. He kept in mind the hospitality she was providing. He felt the best way to reciprocate was to go along with her wishes.

At one of the last tents on the perimeter of the camp, Chamm said, "No goddam women here." He tugged Baxter inside and greeted the three men who were already there, one sandy-haired with a cap and two black-haired men Baxter pegged as Greeks or Italians.

"Don't mean to bust up your sociable," Chamm said. "The wife put us out for a while."

About the stove, the three men sat in a circle which they widened enough for two more crates. Chamm motioned for Baxter to sit.

Eyeing Baxter warily, the capped man said, "*Na co ci tu szef?*"

"*Jest mu teraz gorzej od nas,*" Chamm said.

"What did he say?" Baxter asked.

"Don't worry. He just gets nervous with a boss so close."

"I'm not a boss anymore, not here anyway."

"Ain't that the truth," Chamm said. "I don't guess back home now neither."

"I'm finished with the company."

"Where you gonna catch on next?"

"I haven't the slightest idea."

"Maybe New York could use a good dogholer. Ask around."

"I might need references."

"Tell 'em I sent you."

From beneath the sandy-haired man's chair, a jug of whiskey appeared. Baxter uncorked it, took a pull, and meant to bypass Chamm as he handed it along.

"You better gimmee that jug, Baxter."

"But you don't drink."

"Gimmee it before I bust it over your head. I already had a mama. I ain't looking for another one. Both of us seen enough today to need a drink." Chamm took a deep swallow. "Black times we're living in," he said. He looked around the tent. A box in a corner supported a battered mandolin. Thumbing in its direction, he said, "Santino, how about it?"

One of the black-haired men threw the strap over his shoulder, thought for a moment, and then began to play and sing. His voice was low, mournful, rough.

> *Vidi un teschio sopra un cannone*
> *Fui curioso e gli volli domandare*
> *Esso mi rispose con grande dolore*
> *Morii senza un tocco di campane.*

Chamm closed his eyes, his face an eddy of pleasure and concentration. "Ain't nothin' like a hymn now and again."

"What's he singing?" Baxter asked.

"Shhh."

> *Sono andati, sono andati i miei anni*
> *Sono andati, sono andati, non so dove*
> *Ora che sono arrivato a ottant'anni*
> *Chiamo la vita e la morte mi risponde.*

"It's about an old man. Really old, ready to kick off. It's a nice one."

Baxter felt hollowed out. Having left Chamm's tent before eating, the whiskey roamed at will through his tissues. He was sick of the company, fed up with the strike, and tired of his own disgust. The jug came to him again as a search beam passed overhead, harassing the darkness and creating a pulsing gloom. He thought of the days he'd spent installing the lights on the ridge, working high above the canyons and the plain. Sprawling beyond all of it was his country, but he did not feel a part of it anymore. Too little room was left in all of its expanse for decency. His desires collapsed to the single one of escape. He wanted to board a train with his family. The valley would have to be left to its fate. "I'm sorry," he said softly to Chamm so as not to interrupt the music.

"For what?"

"I failed."

"You ain't the first, Baxter, and you won't be the last. That old rat Robertson screwed you like he done us, but he'd rather climb a tree to tell a lie than stand on the ground and tell the truth. You were never gonna save the world."

"Maybe just this valley."

"A tall order, too tall to reach. The thing we're fightin', you can't ever whip for good. All you can do is keep on swingin' till you're too tired to swing. Then somebody else got to take your place."

"I could have done a better job."

"Leave it be. You did what you could, what you thought was right. That's all you can do. That's all there is."

"That's what Hawkins said."

"True the first time you hear it, true the hunerth."

"He was certainly never at a loss for words."

"He had the gift. I got it for talkin', but he had it for speechin'. He could reach right in and crank your heart. And I'm not talkin' politics. All his hollerin' about the working classes and wages don't move a feather. It's what's underneath that counts. You want action, you need religion, and Hawkins knew how to slide religion into the facts. Debs knows, too."

"Debs again."

"A holy man as sure as I know, but if Hawkins didn't give you the spirit, I ain't gonna try. By and by maybe you come to it yourself." He took another drink. "My face don't hurt so much after a little medicine. Gettin' dizzy with it. Feels good, though. Huh. Time was my family had nothing to do with coal."

"How long ago?"

"Thirty, forty years, but that's nothin' time. Speculators came around soon after the War. They throwed a few hunert bucks to a hillbilly for his mountainful of trees, and it was like Jesus himself brought the pot of manna. You shoulda seen the hills then, Baxter. Hell, *I* shoulda seen 'em, but I gotta go on what Pap told me and imagine the rest. Timber from the foot and up over the spurs and points. Poplars and white oaks down low, chestnuts farther up. Walnut trees everywhere, a yard around. Hickories, maples, basswoods, ash, simmon, black-gum, sycamores, birches, willows. Huge cedars and pines. You could turn your hogs loose in the beeches for the summer, have 'em feed on beechnuts. Seven, eight feet thick for the biggest poplars, two hunert feet high. Not much of it left now. Just pieces. Folks got their land taken for a song. Most hillbillies you could sell a sky hook. Pap was bright, so he held out for a little more money, but they got him in the end. Tough to out-law a speculator."

"I could tell you about buildings, but that's all I have to offer."

"Don't want to hear it. Tell me 'bout streams and moss. Tell me 'bout salamanders and liverwort, rain and ferns, leaves clappin' above my head. I want foamflowers and red catchflies again, orange blooms. That's what I want to hear about. Land that's living, land with guts. The hollers ain't like this valley. This place was shit to start with, ugly from the get-go. The hollers was paradise, but coal's a wrecker, and something you love, something beautiful to start with, when it gets wrecked, you don't take it so easy, 'specially when you're in on the wreckin.' Tell me what living thing you can rip the guts outta without it dyin.'"

"What will you do with Hawkins gone?"

"We'll figure something. We'll hash it out tomorrow. In time we might have to fight, might not. Can't say now."

Baxter looked at him, considering his own words carefully. "How can you fight without weapons?"

Chamm spat on the floor and smeared the blot with his boot. "Things ain't always the way you see 'em." To the blonde man he said, "Ain't that right? *Pozory czasami mylą,*" and the man nodded. "Anyway, it ain't your concern, ain't your fight. Don't think it's going to sort out clear. Sometimes there ain't a clear thing in this world. Don't pay it no mind, though. Get your kin outta here in the morning. That's the best thing. Get out of here and don't look back. You go down in the hollers someday, spread my name around. Find some Champollions. That's the original name. A good number of folks kept it, but my great-great-grandpappy made our line into Chamm. He and his kin wasn't keen on the original since the French and Indian War, but it don't matter either way. You're kin to me now."

"Taking us in tonight," Baxter said, "you don't know what it means to me."

Chamm patted his knee. "Get some music. Try not to think."

The jug came back to him. Baxter didn't drink. His head was already light. He sat for an hour, becoming quiet, listening as Santino played. His hunger ebbed.

In time, Chamm tugged at his elbow. "I reckon it's been long enough. She'll be cooled off by now." They put their coats on and crossed the camp. Chamm waved to whomever they happened to see, and Baxter drew no undue attention. His presence on Chamm's heels apparently removed suspicion. Chamm's footfalls didn't waver in the snow, and Baxter thought of how a loaded train could take miles to come to a full stop, how a long braking gave the impression of uncheckable momentum. He followed Chamm's path, hoping for food, sleep, and escape.

Instead, what they found upon arrival was Garris and Pierce in the tent. Pierce stood in the far corner. Garris sat beside the stove. He touched at his own forehead with a bloody handkerchief. Chamm, puffed with anger, stood over him, threatening. "Maybe nobody told you, nigger, but I don't abide scabs in my home."

Garris, unintimidated, glanced at him and then Pierce. He continued to tend the wound on his head.

"Ask 'em why they're here," Anna said. "Maybe they'll teach your fool head something."

Chamm turned to Pierce. "I don't ask nigger scabs nothin'," he snarled. "I just tell 'em ta git."

Garris said to Pierce, "What I say, huh? What I say 'bout these crackers?"

Pierce said, "Gotta push through it."

"Tell 'em what you told me," Anna said to Garris. He did not acknowledge her. She aimed at her husband. "Go on, ask him why he's here. This valley's a lot bigger than your stinkin' holler, but ain't no room for color here neither. What kind of shadings you ever see in those tunnels? With all that dust, you come home black as a rotted tooth anyway."

Chamm was not swayed. He stood glaring at Garris and Pierce, pushing them out with his eyes. Garris moved toward the exit.

Baxter stuck out his arm and stopped him. "Why are you hurt?"

Garris tossed the handkerchief on the floor. There was a long gash on his forehead. "One of your dagos took a swing at me with a two-by-four. I try to help and I get my head split."

"Help with what?" Baxter said, and again no one answered. He looked from face to silent face. "Help with *what?*"

"Those crates on the ridge," Pierce said.

"Ever get a look in 'em when you was puttin' up them lights?" Garris said.

"We never opened them," Baxter said. "We kept them locked. They're just spare parts."

"Spare parts my ass," Garris said.

Guilt pulled at his ribs. He had lied about his reasons for coming to Colorado. True, the old man had asked him to. False, that he'd been required. He could have refused. Mr. Robertson might not have been adamant. He might have endorsed whomever Baxter suggested in his place, but Baxter never asked, never even considered actions different from obedience.

Colorado beckoned. He was aging. Perhaps half his life or more had passed. He felt a need for adventure. His boyhood was fading, not the events, not the chronology, but rather the feeling, the body-memory of youth. To run without being winded. To fall without fear of injury. The future an unbroken plain of possibility, no mistakes yet made, the material of his life still wet concrete, nothing hardened into permanence. His life-to-come in New York looked as planned and unremarkable as a cobblestone street.

Upon arrival in the desert, black and gray whiskers had sprouted across his jaw. A film of sweat and dust from the plains had coated his face. His jowls and neck sagged with fatigue. An old man's face, he remembered thinking. An old man cheated of his dream, of his calling. An old man who could have become great.

He shifted against the cell wall. Pathetic, he thought. A grown man pining for a lost future. A cliché. Who's to say my future would have been the one I imagined? Childish to demand compliance from the universe. Look how my family paid for my arrogance.

Despair crystallized in him. Old, since to be old means to have burned through the last scraps of life. The proximity of death. In the cell with him and he was not frightened of it. The presence, a thousand times more mundane than he'd been led to believe.

Once, he'd been stuck on a streetcar. He was seated beside an old woman, a stranger, her skin crenellated, thin, the wrinkles like cracks in cheap leather. The car stopped in the middle of a throng. Baxter craned his neck from the window. He could not see the obstruction. An overturned fruit cart? An injured horse? He bristled in his seat. He was late. He wanted to get home. Wordlessly and without looking at him, the old woman patted the top of his hand.

He felt now as he did then. Nothing to do. Simply wait. Soon the world will sort through its present, routine horror. Time and events will reassert themselves, begin moving again.

Come morning, I will no longer move with them, he thought. Death, an old woman who'd once touched his hand. She'd followed him. Now he knew.

20

"Machine guns," Garris said. "That's what's stored up there."

Chamm stepped back. "You sure you saw right?"

"We come off evenin' shift behind the ridge," Pierce said. "Drift-mouth gave a good look up. You could see in the leftover light skittered behind."

"They got one or two guns behind every light," Garris said.

Chamm picked up Garris' handkerchief from the floor and returned it. "You tell anyone else yet?"

"Didn't even point it out to my crew," Garris said, "though I figure most of 'em saw. Pierce and me just headed back to the shack, hashed out what we was going to do about it. We decided to come tell you."

"Glad of that," Chamm said. "Obliged, in fact."

Garris said, "There's a plan." An uninflected question.

"Yup," Chamm said.

"Let's get to it," Pierce said.

"Gotta settle one more thing first," Chamm said.

All three men looked at Baxter.

Chamm said, "No more jawin', boss man. Time to choose up."

A thought came to him as a reflex: They can't be right. But facts had accumulated, ponderous facts. His old faith gave way and fell into the breach. "Tell me what to do."

"First we gotta go around, tell everyone to be ready. We'll leave together. What are your names, anyhow?"

"Pierce. Al Pierce."

"Willie Garris."

Awkwardly, Chamm shook their hands. "You both come around with me. We'll spread word your boys are on board. That's first. Second is a little different, but first is first."

"What about a rally point?" Garris asked.

"Shaft forty-three," Chamm said. "We scouted a weak spot in the fence. Bust it down if you have to. Let's go."

Lorraine rose, facing Baxter for an explanation.

"It's probably nothing," he said, wishing he believed the words himself. "Scare tactics." He indicated Anna. "Do whatever she tells you to do."

~

The men circled through the colony, ducking into tents, Baxter merely standing by as Chamm, in whatever language fit the situation, soothed animosities and spoke of what was to happen. When they finished the rounds, Garris and Pierce slipped back up to the shacks and, parting, Chamm said to them, "Same deal up there. Bring 'em around as best you can." Baxter followed Chamm down Main Street.

"Where are we going?"

"Hush."

No other miners roamed about, and Baxter was already thinking he should have stayed behind. Ahead, two guards walked a patrol. One guard wore a full beard. The other was clean-shaven. The bearded guard looked them up and down. With his rifle, he poked Baxter in the stomach. "Where you goin'?" To Chamm, he said, "This traitor'll turn on you eventually, too, you know."

"Once a traitor, always a traitor," the shaved face said.

Chamm spat to the side, uncowed. "Goin' to the butcher shop. We heard there's some old meat in the trash around back. One of our guys saw it gittin' pitched earlier today. Gonna scrounge it."

The flatness of the answer stymied the guards.

"That all right?" Chamm continued with more indignance. "That all right we get some rotten meat for our young'uns, or you prefer we starve and freeze at the same time?"

The beard said, "I don't need your hillbilly sass," but he stepped aside and allowed them to move on.

Baxter whispered, "What are you talking about?"

Chamm ignored him. At the butcher shop, they went around to the alley in the rear where trash cans lined the wall. "Open 'em up," Chamm said. "Make a little noise while you're doing it. And don't ask nothin' about it. Just keep at it. We need to make a show."

They opened the cans and rummaged. The metal clanged as Chamm worked his way down the row toward the last can near the service door. "See anybody?"

Baxter looked about. "No one."

Chamm slipped a key from his pocket and opened the door. Baxter followed him inside. Chamm turned on the single bulb in the storeroom and opened the industrial freezer. Sides of beef hung from the ceiling. A wooden crate lay along the rear wall. Chamm lifted the lid. Baxter saw various cuts of meat wrapped and labeled. Chamm tossed these packages out on the floor. "Come on and help. We need to get this done quick."

The meat was heavy, and Baxter was soon warm with exertion even in the frigid temperature. When the crate was empty, they moved it into the storeroom, whereupon Chamm went to a corner and pushed a table aside. He knelt down and stuck his finger into a knot in the wood. He pulled, and a section of the floor lifted away. Seamed by the ends of individual planks and lacking any handle, the section was perfectly camouflaged. Chamm thrust his arm into the hold, and his hand came up with an aged rifle, then another, and again. He moved with haste but also with caution and efficiency as he set the rifles beside the hole. "Put 'em in the crate." He dredged up handguns, boxes of ammunition.

Baxter had trouble believing what he was seeing, what he was doing. "Those guns on the train, you said they weren't yours."

"They wasn't. These here are ours. This ain't all of 'em, neither."

"How did you get so many past Lind?"

"One here, one there. It stacks up after a while. The butcher's a sympathizer."

Baxter stopped loading the weapons. "Wait."

"For what?" Chamm said, his voice harsh and abrupt.

Baxter picked up a rifle and held it out. "Show me how to use it."

Chamm stood up. "It's what they call a trapdoor model." Demonstrating, he lifted the breech and took a cartridge from the ammunition, dropping it in place. "Just close the trapdoor," he said, shutting the breech, "and it's loaded." He feinted aim and handed it back to Baxter. "Just fire after that."

"Where did it come from?"

"Union bought up surplus after the Spanish-American War. Military don't use these anymore. They got Krag-Jorgensens now. A better model. I always wanted one. Too expensive. If we get in a scrape, that's what they'll come at us with, I think. Maybe Spanish Mausers, too. But the trapdoor is a good gun for us. Runs on blackpowder, which we got plenty of. Watch out for the smoke, though. It'll give your position away."

"What's the range on it?"

"Couldn't say exactly. Aim careful. It ain't too accurate until you get used to it." Chamm picked up a pistol. He checked to ensure it was empty, then pulled back the hammer. "This one, you just cock it and fire." He pulled the trigger to a loud click. "Just like that." He loaded the chambers and dropped the pistol into one pocket of Baxter's overcoat. A handful of bullets went into another. Chamm supplied himself likewise. "Just a precaution, like you said." A steady clunking filled the room until the cavity was empty and the crate was full. They pushed it outside.

"Hey!" A guard stepped from under the eave of a building at the far end of the alley. He came forward, rifle leveled.

Baxter cursed. "What do we do now?"

"Don't know."

The guard's face was smooth, unstubbled, skinny, youthful. And frightened. Baxter said, "He's just a kid."

Chamm whispered, "Keep your yap shut for a second." He called out, "Don't you never talk to your bosses?"

The boy was upon them. "How's that?"

"We already went through this with a couple of your buddies. We're scrounging food."

"What were you doing inside?"

"Door was open, so we brung out this here crate of rotten meat. Gonna pick through it, see what we can salvage."

The boy's eyes brushed from Baxter to Chamm and back again.

"Don't believe me?" Chamm said. "Go ahead and look for yourself. Mind the maggots, though. Slimy little critters."

The boy's rifle angled away as he turned his attention to the crate. He lifted the lid, and almost faster than Baxter could register it, Chamm took out his pistol, buried it in the boy's abdomen and fired. Baxter gasped. The clothing and flesh muffled the shot, but as the boy folded to the ground, an errant shot, loud as a cannon, escaped the rifle.

The boy was not dead. He lay moaning and gurgling on the ground. Chamm took his rifle and slung it over his own shoulder. He squatted down. "Awful sorry. Had to do it. Hated to do it. Spell your name to God now, son. It'll soon be over."

The boys eyes were wet and pried open with terror. He was unable even to cry out.

Chamm hooked his hands under the boy's armpits. "Got him through the liver, I think," Chamm said. "Bad way to go. Hum-up there, Baxter. Help me. Grab his feet."

Revulsion wormed through Baxter's skin as he took the boy's ankles. "Where to?"

"Stick him in the storeroom. He can scream his head off in there if he takes a mind to."

"Holy God," Baxter choked as he helped to carry the warm, writhing weight indoors.

"Ain't a time to go soft now," Chamm said. "Soon as he got a look in that crate, the war was on. Nothing to stop it. Just gotta do it. Bad luck killed that boy, but bad luck'll kill you good as anything else."

They dropped the boy and closed the door as they left. He's alone in there, Baxter thought as cylinders of light scurried across the town, searching from the ridges for the source of the shot.

"See? Bad luck, Baxter. Time ta git."

They dashed from the alley, crossing through the line of buildings and into the street, moving back toward the camp. A pillar of light attached itself to them, tracked their path, and a line of small white puffs erupted from the snow only yards ahead. Chamm grabbed Baxter's arm and almost ripped it loose as he pulled him into a dodging retreat. Softened by distance came the tack-tack-tack of a machine gun. The initial burst released a cascade of fire from the other ridges. Baxter heard screams and the pounding of feet as the guns poured ordnance into the town and the camp.

In the alley again, Chamm tore at the lid of the crate and extracted two rifles, shoving one into Baxter's arms. Both men climbed the fire escape to the roof of the butcher shop and found cover behind a high balustrade. Chamm said, "The lights," and leaned out only far enough to aim and fire. Baxter fumbled with his rifle, but somehow a round found its way into the chamber. He leaned out, too, half conscious from panic. He fired, pulled the bolt, and fired again with no confidence in his aim. Chamm somehow mustered the restraint to set up his shots with some stability. Soon one of the lights exploded. The moon and still-living searchlights revealed white men pounding away from the camp and across the street. On the downslopes of the bluffs: black men. Some were cut down. Others escaped. In the alley, footsteps scurried and the crate slammed and slammed as strikers armed themselves.

More shots flew to the ridge, and the lights began to wink out. Two to the north, another to the south, and then another. As if coordinated, the remaining beams lost their vitality. The spots fell motionless in single places. "Lind's bringing the lightmen down now," Chamm said. He rose and made for the edge of the building. Baxter did not follow. "Come on now, Baxter." His legs would not obey. Chamm yanked him to his feet, and Baxter's puttied legs somehow found integrity and function. At the fire escape, a guard crested the facade. Baxter drew his pistol and shot him dead. A reflex. No hesitation. Like a loose brick, the body fell into the alley. Chamm and Baxter hurried down the ladder, Baxter's mind treadmilling the image of the falling guard.

Without the searchlights to guide them, the unceasing machine guns faltered for aim. Chamm gained the buildings on the far side of the street. Gunfire had shredded the cheap canvas of the tents. Fires had broken out from upset stoves and oil lamps, and toward the perimeter, guards helped the colony alight with torches.

Running in leaps, Baxter was suddenly covered with blood. He fell back howling, clawing at himself, thinking he had been shot, but to his side Chamm was on the ground. His chest lay open as if a fist had punched through from within. Baxter, gagging, scrambled back between the buildings again, tripping and falling over himself as he retreated. Shaking, he dropped behind a barrel and pulled his knees into his chest. Behind him, shrieks and gunshots crescendoed and merged with the roar of the tent fires which created their own wind, drawing in air and stoking the camp.

Baxter clamped his eyes shut only to see Chamm fall again and again. Strikers ran past, some singly, some in groups of five or six, a mixture of men and women, both dragging children not already clinging to them. He scanned frantically, hoping for a glimpse of Lorraine and Thomas. No one noticed him crouched against the building. Men ran, fired back at the guards who pursued them, fell dead, killed, and moved toward the mines.

Baxter could not force himself into motion. A boy about Thomas' age, lagging his mother as she ran, paused before the barrel and looked at him. The boy's mother stopped, came back with another child in her arms, then pulled the boy on. At last, Baxter darted for Chamm's tent. The fire was stupefyingly hot, the center of the camp a cauldron. The flames had already burned through the perimeter tents. Of Chamm's, only the frame remained standing, bits of smoldering canvas clinging to it like leaves. Baxter threw himself on what was left of the flooring, singeing his hands on the charred wood. He clawed for the trap door and tumbled into the earth.

The cavity was bizarrely calm. Above, the air periodically rent with bullets. Beneath the ground, he was shielded. And not alone. In the flaring light he saw the four bodies, peaceful and blue-hued, black soot gathered around their nostrils and lips. They were huddled together in repose. No wounds nor burns marred them. The fire had stolen their air and had left them behind. Mute, he took Lorraine's hand, still warm but without the spring of life. Thomas curled in her lap, warm, too, limp and quiet as a small sack of grain. Baxter took up the boy and cradled him, weeping, kissing his smoke-rank hair and skin. Anna and Oliver, likewise, monstrously serene and gone. He rested Thomas with his mother again and drew away, falling to all fours, ruptured with uncontrollable sobs. Grief crushed his abdomen. The dirt and rocks gouged under his fingernails. He tore at himself, forehead to the ground. His wet lips fouled with soil, yet a piston of instinct, sick-making, self-preserving instinct, shot up through his sorrow. *If they find me here, they will kill me, too.* He shoved back his agony and pushed away from the ground. He kissed all four bodies goodbye.

He climbed up through the trap. He moved sluggishly at first and then ran, flying in what felt like five- and six-step strides. He swam the orange light of flash and flame with long, panic-strong strokes. Wherever he saw a uniform, he fired. Later in the mine he would realize he'd emptied his pistol. He fled toward the bluffs, running until he lost feeling in his legs. Time shot and held, shot and held. His lungs and throat roasted in acidic heat. He kept going. Centuries passed before he reached shaft forty-three.

He reached back to his old life, to his life before his crimes, the life recognizable as such, not the miasma into which it had been transformed. He saw his present self through bad glass. Before, times of clarity. Walking by the door to the washroom. The sound of water dripping into the basin.

"Harlan?"

He came a few steps back, opened the door only far enough to hear her clearly.

"I forgot a towel. Can you get me one?"

"Of course."

He went to the closet across the hall. He opened the door again, held the towel aloft.

"Put it on the basin stand, please. I can't reach it from here."

Baxter came in. She did not bother to look over her shoulder. He closed the door as if he had left. Her back to him, she gave no impression of suspecting his presence. Still afternoon. She had not switched on the light. No need. Plenty of sun in the room.

Her long dark hair lay slicked to where it ended halfway down her back. Small bubbles of soap clung to each strand. With a pitcher, she dipped water from the basin and rinsed herself. Shimmering, braided water fell in thick threads down her skin.

"Do you need anything else, miss?"

She pivoted with a jolt.

Baxter rose. He kissed her bare shoulder, the base of her neck. He tasted the residue of lye.

"Thomas will hear," she said.

"We'll just have to be quiet."

They took each other with wonderful, muffled joy. Baxter's hands fumbled, slipping as he held her soap-slick body against his own.

Sigh now and remember soft flesh beneath hands, cooled water on skin giving way to live heat.

I have committed no crimes.

21

He couldn't remember how many bodies he passed along the way. The fencing around the driftmouth had been battered down, and as he lunged into the shaft, shots sped past him from its throat. Baxter ran on, uncomprehending of the miners who'd taken up positions inside the tunnel to fire at guards who tried to enter. Dead men littered the fence and the driftmouth. Later, Garris told him his bloody clothes had saved him. "They figured you for a miner. Blood's the badge."

The shaft led to a large stope where other survivors huddled in the dark, crying and whispering. Baxter staggered in, wide-eyed and dumb with shock. Garris and Pierce and some of their comrades had survived, many of the wives and children, too. Amid a genderless weeping and moaning, some like Baxter, lapsed terrified into silence.

In ones and twos, more people arrived. Soon the trickle diminished to nothing. Movement commenced. Deeper into the mine. Turn now right, now left. Finally, they stopped, and all quieted. Pierce's voice asserted itself. "Time come 'round for us, Willie. Our chance now."

Garris moved to Baxter, who had settled onto his knees against the rock wall. He could not stop trembling. He had never run as far nor as hard as he had to reach the tunnel. For all he knew, his heart might collapse from the stress. His family dead. Chamm dead. Chamm's family dead. The people in the pit were not known to him because he did not know people to whom such things happen. He looked at Garris, into his headlamp. He clutched himself as if he might burst apart. He felt Garris' hand on his shoulder.

"We safe here?" Garris asked.

Still shaking, Baxter only stared. Garris stepped away. "We safe here?" he repeated. He waited for an answer. Baxter couldn't speak.

Garris leveled him with a leaden, open-handed, sweeping blow.

Baxter rolled with a white flash. The left side of his head stung and grew hot. In moments, he sat up straight again, his body humming with offense. Garris stooped beside him and peered without cruelty into his face. "You all right now?"

Baxter had stopped trembling.

"I gotta know," Garris said. "You the only boss. Are they gonna blow these tunnels around us or what?"

Baxter knew the answer, and the confidence with which he knew it set him tottering on the edge of a great, dark hole. "No," he said. "First, coal. Second, equipment. Third, mules. Fourth, men. The company isn't going to bring the investment down on our heads. But they might send the guards in."

"Those guards ain't comin', leastways not now."

"How we know that?" Pierce said.

"Too many of them dead by the mouth already. They're not gonna risk it. They don't know their way around. They'll sit us out a spell."

"Better be right," Pierce said.

"Amen," Garris said.

Hours passed. Baxter waited for further tears that refused to erupt. At last, he said, "Someone should go and see what's happening outside." He heard his own monotone, the thoughts somehow speaking themselves. "Someone should check."

No one responded. Garris only watched him.

Baxter rose mechanically to his feet. "Tell me the way."

"Depends on where you want to come out," Garris said.

"Somewhere high. Remote."

"Come on."

Baxter held the tail of Garris' shirt as they walked into the darkness of an adjacent tunnel. "Try and remember the turns," Garris said. "Where we goin' from where we started is two rights first, then a left."

"Two rights and a left," Baxter said.

They slowed, creeping toward a driftmouth. A circle of stars appeared. The cold air from the surface met them. They didn't see any guards. Only the main shafts were numbered, and Lind didn't have the manpower to cover the myriad smaller entrances. At the driftmouth, dirt gave way to undisturbed snow. No corpses, no footprints, no sign of conflict. Nevertheless, they waited for a long time before emerging.

The tunnel emptied high above shaft forty-three where the trampled fencing and bloody snow shone in the moonlight. On the plain, individual tent fires had mostly burned themselves out. One large bonfire glowed where guards delivered the remains of the camp to the pyre. Perhaps fifty strikers who had not reached the shelter of the mines were cordoned at gunpoint near the camp, and just beyond its perimeter, other guards hacked out a large hole in the ground with picks or shovels. The surrounding snow was already clodded with dirt.

"Ground's gotta be like brick. Helluva chore choppin' a grave outta that," Garris said. "Gonna be a big one, too."

"Yes," Baxter said.

"We should go back in now, figure what to do."

Baxter did not reply, riveted by the digging.

Garris nudged him. "What's next ain't somethin' we can decide on our own. We gotta talk it over. Come on, go on in."

Baxter led the return trip so as to learn the way. In the meeting room, he sat down among expectant faces. Baxter opened his mouth to speak but then remembered Chamm no longer accompanied him.

"English?" he asked roundly, hoping for at least one vessel of fluency. A few faces merely twisted with sympathy.

He drew in the dirt with his finger. A stick figure with bosoms and long hair. A much smaller figure beside her. "Women and children," he said to no one in particular. Garris joined in, drawing a driftmouth and figures leaving it. Above, Baxter wrote a large question mark and waited for an answer from the others. A squat man with black matted hair pushed forward. He circled the exit drawing and drew a gravestone next to it.

Garris considered the gravestone. "You think that's what's waitin' for 'em?"

"I don't know," Baxter said. Just then desperate tears pushed up through him. He tamped them down. "How can I know that?"

Garris wiped his hands on his thighs. "Let's think this out. If they don't start shootin', then what?"

"They'll be arrested for certain, then shipped back to Denver. After that, who knows?"

"Guards already got some folks gathered up. You saw them from up top. They'd be dead already if Lind wanted it, so maybe they ain't killin' if you surrender. Ain't no way to know, is there?"

"No."

Garris drew another large question mark over the gravestone. The others murmured.

Baxter said, "I'm not leaving."

"I know," Garris said.

"What about us, Willie?" Pierce asked.

"Dunno. What's your feeling on it?"

"We run here, we just gonna have to keep runnin'."

"So, most of us leave, but some stay behind," Baxter said. "How long can we hold out?"

Garris and Pierce exchanged a look. Pierce said to Baxter, "I got word to Hawkins a couple times about what we seen down here in these tunnels. A body stumbles on a lot, goin' round on shifts. He tell you we talked?"

"Not a word."

"Good man," Garris said with respect. "Thing is, these tunnels are full up with lots more than coal. We can make a hell of a mess if we want, but how long we hold out depends on how many stay."

"Twenty-five," Baxter guessed. "Maybe thirty-five."

"This ain't bullshit, Baxter. I seen plenty of what we're talkin' about, more than you know. You go in for this, you better know what it means."

"What do I have left?" Baxter said.

Garris rose stiffly to his feet, pointed toward an exit tunnel. In the dirt he drew a long, leading arrow. Ten feet away, Baxter laid his pistol on the ground and sat down behind it. The women and children moved toward the exit tunnel while the male survivors made their choices.

"Stay or go," Garris spoke to himself, "Stay or go."

Baxter could not bear the sorrow of the farewells. He walked farther into the earth and waited in the darkness until someone came to fetch him. In the end, Garris, Pierce, and twenty-eight others had sat down behind the pistol.

Garris whistled once for the attention of those gathered by the exit tunnel. He swept a hand over his own group. "All of us," he said, and drew a finger across his neck. "Tell 'em ain't nobody left in here."

Heads nodded in the departing crowd.

"'Specially him," Garris said, pointing at Baxter. "He was shot on the way and died in here."

Baxter splayed himself out for effect.

More nods, and then, weeping, the others walked up the exit tunnel.

"You think they understood?"

"Better hope so," Garris said.

They posted sentries for the night. Each man took a rifle or a pistol and headed into a different tunnel. Baxter and Garris climbed back to the high driftmouth and watched the column of survivors empty onto the plain, watched as they joined the existing prisoners. Baxter and Garris alternated sleeping for an hour each until dawn. A train arrived. The prisoners were loaded aboard and were shipped from the valley. Baxter sent an empty prayer after them. He and Garris watched the train shrink to invisibility in the distance.

"That's a lot of folks with eyes full up from this place."

Baxter said, "Surrender was their best shot. But Lind can't believe we're all dead."

"He got nothin' to lose by waiting." Garris said. "If we ain't here, good for him. If we are, he just keeps waitin'."

"Until we starve."

"Uh huh. 'Cept we ain't gonna starve," Garris said.

They rotated the sentries, and Garris took the other men through the mines. They spread out, uncovering supplies, food under old and discarded carts, weapons and ammunition tucked into obscure crevices. The tunnels, a secret market of candles, spare helmet lamps, stashes of blackpowder, fuses, dried beans, and pasta.

"Water," Baxter said.

Another tunnel, a hot tunnel, led to a spring and a pool on the floor. Baxter knelt and drank. Later, resting, chewing dry lentils, discussion opened. A few words of English, hardly anything that could be called speech, began to sketch a map to translation. A blonde man among them explained an idea. He drew train tracks in the dirt, then a bridge. He mouthed an explosion and erased the bridge.

"Where?" Garris asked.

The blonde man looked at Baxter.

"The Arkansas River," Baxter said. "At Pueblo. We stopped there on our trip in. I remember because the engineer woke me up with the announcement. It was the halfway point to Denver."

"A hundred miles," Garris said. "He can't make it that far."

Baxter wrote 100 MILES on the ground, and beside that, 160 KILO-METERS.

The blonde man nodded, looking at the figures.

Garris caught his attention and then shivered theatrically.

The man pointed proudly to himself. "Norveejun," he said.

"Snow, cold, and dark," Garris said. "Guess you're used to 'em."

They loaded him with clothes and lentils and enough blackpowder for the demolition. He took a pistol and ammunition. Once beyond the town limits, he would need only to follow the tracks north across the desert. He made snowshoes from two planks, bindings with wire.

When he was ready, he waited for night and followed a tunnel emptying into the fringe of the canyons. He would sweep wide beyond town before turning north. They all shook his hand, wished him good luck. The Norwegian said, "You eight days wait," and vanished into the cold.

For the next days and nights, sentries watched for a pursuit party and saw nothing. In the meantime, the holdouts planned, fashioned their supplies, made their first attempts at explaining themselves. Sometimes hours passed before a man could make his story clear. No matter. Time enough. Nothing but time. Baxter listened to the voices in the dark.

On the ninth day, Pierce said, "Either way, Norway's in the promised land now. Time to heat up this valley."

He looked through the hole in the wall again and could no longer see the moon. Past the zenith, he thought. The moon rolls down the sky, pulls up dawn. Less time than ever now. Memories of beginnings.

From the depot, little to see. Stunted cedars and piñon pines and the high desert landscape of sage. "Is everything here?"

Lorraine tallied their baggage. "It looks so."

A child's arms around his leg. He smoothed the boy's hair as the boy looked up and yawned. No crowds pressed them as at the city stations. Only three other passengers had traveled this far, three filthy, sullen men who quickly disappeared from the platform. Miners, no doubt. New recruits or old hands? The trip had tired him beyond caring. That said, he was eager for work, glad to have arrived so that work could begin.

From New York the train clattered into Chicago and through Illinois and Iowa. Nebraska ensued, a long gradient of corn to grass. His first time so far west, the plains hypnotized him. He stared for hours at the bright line of the Platte, then the sweeping turn south into eastern Colorado. They made the Denver transfer near midnight, all three of them half asleep. He was amazed they arrived on time. He stretched his back, and it popped loudly with stiffness.

Heat-shimmers and dust shrouded the low-slung town. Behind it rose a sloping wall of crenellated bluffs.

"I suppose it could be worse," Lorraine said.

Lind showed them about. Main Street, a dirt track. A saloon here, a supply house there. Everything constructed in two- and three-story clapboard. A post office near the driftmouth of one of the mines. Off-shift miners lingered. If every one of them had told me the truth, I would not have believed it. I had to see for myself, become someone other than myself in order to learn.

"We have some nice quarters set up for you," Lind said. A mile between the house and the town. The house, recently whitewashed. Lind walked them around the property, showed them the tool shed, the outhouse, the outdoor shower. Lind's men delivered their wicker trunks, footlocker, hanging closet. The artifacts of custom.

"I hope we didn't forget anything," Lorraine said, kneeling by a half empty trunk. "I hate being rushed."

"I wouldn't worry. I doubt people here are concerned with fashion."

"Did you hear what Mr. Lind said about the weather? Maybe we didn't bring enough warm clothes."

Baxter opened another suitcase. "I'll requisition an extra uniform for you."

"Don't joke, Harlan. This isn't exactly easy for me."

"I'm sorry, love. I know it isn't." He sat down beside her on the floor and stroked her back. "You know this wasn't my first choice."

He went downstairs in search of celebratory liquor. In the kitchen, a full tinderbox and water keg. In the cabinets, enough cookware for six people, a fully stocked refrigerator. A marvel. He hadn't yet replaced their icebox in Brooklyn. A pint bottle of whiskey in a cupboard above the stove. Thank you, Mr. Robertson, he muttered. He scraped the wax from the bottle, filled a glass halfway to the brim. Through the window above the sink spread a black night-plain to the south.

22

An unguarded driftmouth near a group of large slag piles. The slag piles along the patrol route. At night, the shaft was scouted, the patrol, timed. Eight men for the operation. One by one, they ran and buried themselves in the slag. The patrol passed and Baxter ran. The mass of rock, surprisingly pliant. He dropped to the ground and stretched out against the pile, burrowing in. He was black with coal dust, a shard broken from the night. By the time the patrol approached again, the small avalanches of rock had settled.

The patrol passed. The next man positioned himself.

Not hard to count to the end. Footsteps clearly audible, regimented and calm in the guards' case, scurrying and animal-like among the others.

Five.

Wait. Wait. Wait.

Six.

Baxter held his pistol in his right hand. He had barely pulled it beneath the surface of rock. His hand began to sweat. His mind turned with rehearsal.

Seven.

No bodies would be retrieved. No time. Whoever was shot, whoever fell, would remain where he lay.

Eight.

All in now. Wait for the next cycle.

The calm footsteps came again, then passed.

Roll.

Kneel.

The air roared with light and sound. The pistol leaped and grew hot and then spat only dull clicks. He was running. The patrol was down. Not even enough time to turn and identify the attackers. I've shot someone in the back and killed him. A dry thought, inert and incontrovertible. The men in the patrol, dead. He and the others, still alive. Lind would very soon know both facts.

He kept running.

They never again used so many men at once. Surprise could no longer camouflage them. Instead they worked in pairs and alone. A pistol, a rifle, four blackpowder bombs each for a raid. Their clothing, a cloak of innumerable tunnels which the old man would not allow Lind to destroy. Men were replaceable. Coal was limited, valuable.

~

Pierce said, "We need extras."

"I can't run with more than four. They'll be too heavy," Baxter said. He tied off the fuse he was working on, joining four bombs together. He handed the assembly to Pierce and started on his own duplicate.

"You rather run slow with enough, or run quick and be short?"

"I'd rather run *and* be loaded," Baxter said. "Willie, how many small ones do we have? No better target for them than this."

A candle blazed dangerously in a far corner. Garris counted ten smaller charges, harder to build than the larger bombs. Baxter didn't ask for them lightly. Garris brought them close and split the supply between Baxter and Pierce.

"Blow 'em up right," Garris said.

"We ain't gonna waste 'em," Pierce said.

"Best not," Garris said. "I'd come along, but I can't run like I used to. You don't need me slowin' you down. Figure how I see both of you again, though."

"Don't sweat it," Pierce said. He took up his sack of bombs, as did Baxter. They exited behind the slag piles which shielded an approach to the tipple. They counted eight guards outside the complex.

"How far from here to there?" Pierce said.

"A hundred yards, maybe a hundred and fifty. How the hell are we going to do this?"

Pierce rested on one knee and thought. "Can you shoot straight?"

"Straight enough."

"Maybe we can hit two right off with the rifles. We toss a smallie that way"—he pointed to a far slag pile—"behind there, see. They'll look that way while we line up and pot 'em. There'll be more smoke from the bomb than from the rifles, and if a couple of them run that way, could be enough time to get inside, do what we came for."

As Pierce spoke, Baxter listened, knowing he would soon carry out exactly the actions described. The certainty of that thought took him out of himself. "What happens if we get inside and there are ten of them in there?"

"Then, been nice knowing you, Mr. Baxter." In a high whisper, Pierce crooned, "Time's flyin', niggers dyin', the judgment of the Lord comin' down."

Baxter said, "Stop that."

"Sorry, boss. Just tryin' ta lighten the mood a little."

"Drop the rifle after the first shot," Baxter said. "You got your pistol?"

"Give you one guess."

The moment before the plunge. Baxter breathed harder. Pierce, too, became grave. His body tensed. Baxter took one of the small charges from his own supply. He squatted and chambered a round in his rifle. He picked up the charge again. His hand was shaking. "You want to throw it or should I?"

"You."

Baxter lit the match and touched it to the fuse. The tiny waterfall of sparks commenced. He threw the bomb as far as he could. He breathed out to steady himself, then lifted the rifle to his shoulder.

An explosion. A concussive wave. Slag and smoke filled the air. Baxter and Pierce fired once each, and two guards fell. Three others plunged away toward the explosion, but the other three remained. Baxter crashed into the lead, his pistol already out. He did not look behind him. Ahead, one of the guards stumbled backward. His head slammed into the side of the building. Baxter couldn't tell whether he fell dead or merely unconscious.

Baxter changed direction at random while still closing distance. Light escaped the rifle muzzles of the two remaining guards. Baxter aimed a shot on the run. One of the men dropped, screaming with a shattered shoulder. He knocked into his partner. Distraction enough. Baxter passed the corner of the building, devoid of more guards. A large sliding door stood open to the tipple.

Baxter dashed inside where the shaker screens continued to run. He navigated through the noise and dust to the generator, hulking grayly and thrumming at the north end of the long building. No one on his heels. Pierce should be following, he thought. He fleeted to his target. Still no pursuing sounds. Just the humming of the dynamo and the monotonous pounding of the sorting machinery.

He took out the bomb assemblage and laid it down, wedging the explosives as deeply as he could into the viscera of the generator. He spooled out the long fuse. Now he heard it: pursuit by the door as he struck a match. A shot ricocheted from the generator, pinging the steel above his head. He touched the match to the fuse and ran. His right arm burned suddenly with pain. He dropped the pistol. He was outside again, in flight again. Ahead, the slag piles lay an impossible distance away, mirage-like in their inaccessibility.

He felt the explosion rather than heard it. A seismic wave rippled across the snow and broke on the slag. He lunged forward for cover, stumbling still toward the mines, glancing back as the north side of the tipple burst with spears of fire and sparks that threw orange light on Pierce's body, its face shot away, its limbs splayed with interrupted motion. Baxter cried out unintelligibly in the dark as the electrical grid sputtered off through town. He dropped into the throat of the mine and threw himself prone. Nothing. No pursuers. Still, he waited, gasping for breath, clearing space for his enflamed lungs until he was able to stand again. Something dripped on his boot. He attempted a fist with his right hand and his arm sung with pain. He struck a match. A red hole glared at him from just below his elbow. He limped back into the earth, to the common room.

"Nobody with you," Garris said.

"No."

Garris looked down. He cleared his throat with difficulty. "Ain't that somethin'."

"He saved my life," Baxter said. "If I'd had one more guard to deal with . . ."

Garris coaxed a lantern into flame. "Hitch up your sleeve," he said.

Baxter said, "I'm sorry."

"Just hitch up your sleeve."

With a canteen, Garris poured water over the wound, and Baxter inhaled sharply as the water collided with his opened flesh. Blood and dirt flushed away. Garris dabbed him with a scrap of cloth. "Took a hunk out of you. Punched straight through. I'll tie it up."

Garris snatched an old shirt from amongst his bedding and tore off a rough bandage. He wrapped it around Baxter's arm but did not cinch it down. "You ready?" Baxter took a deep breath, steeling himself, and he choked off a scream as Garris snapped the knot tight.

"Keep washin' it out."

"I'm sorry," Baxter prodded again.

"You got your blood," Garris said, breaking. "Hope it heals you." He vaporized alone into a tunnel. Baxter did not follow. On the surface, no more telegraph, no more lights, no more power. Darkness swallowed the valley. The night was complete.

~

After the tipple, they prioritized. Water first. Without the generator, all pumps fell idle. Lind would have to rely on the water tower. Two Italians volunteered to destroy it. That night, Baxter was working in the tunnels when he heard the echo of an explosion. Daylight revealed a collapsed and emptied tower. The Italians never returned.

"Lind and his boys'll have snow for a while," Garris said. "But we hang on until summer and they die of thirst."

Next, food. A two-week operation. Five cycles of two men, different for each raid to the bakery, the commissary, the butcher shop. All blown up and torched. Liquor not pinched from the saloons burned with blue and pink flames. The strikers did not relent. Lind did not relent. Baxter longed for a clear shot at him, but the opportunity never presented itself. Bombs detonated the office, imploded and choked off the wells. Twenty heavy charges annihilated the coke ovens and sent a fireball skyward like the world was made of hay and kerosene. The carcass of the tipple leaned precipitately north, an elephant with its front legs blasted away.

Between raids, they waited as long as possible. Days, sometimes a week or two. Anything to give the impression that the most recent raid had been the final one, that all attackers had starved at last. No danger in delay. No trains arrived with supplies nor reinforcements. Either the Norwegian had succeeded or the old man had put through a simple order to wait. Baxter understood the calculation. If local men couldn't solve the problem, the governor and president stood ready to assist. The old man, when he called, would not be refused. Why not exhaust his private options before asking for help? To do otherwise might indicate a lack of resolve. To do otherwise would be bad business. In the end, the coal would survive.

Through the days, they gathered and talked in the darkness. Dead headlines breathed of labor and lives everywhere in flames. Baxter made his powder bombs and chewed his lentils and listened. Time stretched and recoiled, spread its passage thin to vanishing and then vanished. He grasped the present day. He was not wounded again, though the wound on his arm refused to heal. He washed and wrapped it only to see it mend partially and flare again. In times when his arm approached its old functioning, he grew expert at loading rifles, attaching fuses. Then night came and all the willing swam into the dark water. Some returned while one or two more bodies shifted residence to the plain, the rubble, the driftmouths. Somehow Baxter persisted.

Nights. Days.

Now and then, snow.

Days and nights.

Eventually, fewer men occupied the tunnels.

Eventually, fewer men occupied the plain.

Eventually, the snow melted and disappeared.

A man's character is his fate. But not this character, not this fate. All is flux. Change is possible, given time. I have no time. I have changed enough already. I am a criminal, my old life the record of my crimes. My cowardice and weakness, my self-regard and scaled eyes. My obedience is at issue, my credulity, my cultivation and civilized manner, my competence, my professional rectitude. Savageries. They demand explanation. I cannot explain. I cannot absolve myself. I reached limits. I could not endure without retribution. I learned the limits of retribution itself.

He picked at the floor, pried loose a long splinter that he spun between his thumb and forefinger and flicked through the bars. The splinter bounced end-over-end, came to rest near the desk. Speculation of cleanup carried him away. The jail, repaired, the roof, patched, the floors, swept, replanked. The splinter would move from dustpan to plain, would be lost with the old flooring. Scrap wood. Fuel. Perhaps material to cap another burning mine. More men trapped. Perhaps not.

No end. Miners and officials would return, different from those before. The coal, still here. People would return for it. Time would move on. He would not be a part of it. Time would move on and Garris and the others might, too. Then time would move on again and they would not either.

The past lingers in the present only partially visible, partially under-stood. He imagined a scenario of escape. Somehow burying the rage. A life in a new city. A new name. A new family. Twenty years might pass before he told anyone his story. Fallen days. Days of desperation and division. Days of roars and dispossession. A blackened time. I tell you it existed. I lived through it. I participated. Go to the valley, smell the blood in the soil. He could admonish, command. He wouldn't, not even if he got the chance. The uncomprehending stares, more infuriating than bullets. Garris and the others would carry the story, save it from myth. Never history, for history owes nothing to those who notice it. Memory, punishment and an indifferent passing.

He picked another splinter from the floor, rolled it, flicked it away.

23

From behind a boulder, Baxter scanned the ruins of the valley. Only patches of snow remained on the plain. In town, wrecked buildings smoldered and popped. The charred remnants of the tent city ebbed in mud. The guard's camp had been much reduced, though it remained intact, having shrunk with each guard killed. All was a residue of what it had once been. Baxter scratched at his beard. "How many left out there, do you think?"

Garris counted. "Eight tents. Figure four men each."

"And we?"

"Ten men. Guns and bullets are runnin' low. Plenty of blackpowder, but there ain't much left to use it on."

Garris' starved-down and sinking face rendered his eyes great-orbited as they blossomed and wilted with pulses of thought. Baxter looked at the tissues of filth masquerading as his own clothes. An abyss of sadness moved into him. "I heard them again last night, screaming, coughing."

"You need to put all that away from you."

"How?"

"No idea, but that load ain't one you chose. Company chose it for you."

Baxter was quiet.

"Did you hear me?"

"Yes."

Garris dug his heel into the ground and turned his foot back and forth. "How long you think he'll wait?"

"Not much longer now. Once spring dries everything out, he'll take the next step. For all we know he had that bridge fixed months ago."

"Why didn't he come?"

"Maybe there was a coal surplus this winter," Baxter said. "Keeping product off the market drives up the price."

Garris harrumphed. "Let's hole up, think on how to finish off."

They joined the others in the sleeping chamber. Garris, too tired to follow his own suggestion, fell quickly to snoring. Baxter remained awake. He lay still and thinking. Perhaps an hour passed before he rose again, careful not to disturb the others. The stope pulsed with breath. He climbed to the ridge through tunnels different from the ones they typically followed to lookouts. From where he crouched, he could see the remains of the office. He'd brought along a blanket. Continuously cold, he'd grown as thin as a consumptive. His blood was airy from near starvation. He wrapped the blanket around himself, gathering the scaffolding of his body so the wind would not blow it down.

He surveilled the town, watching the remnant clusters of guards, marking their movements and positions. Since the first raid, Lind had randomized the patrols, leaving no way to predict a precise pattern, but the guards' numbers were so diminished that long gaps stretched between passings. Baxter scratched in the dirt to plan his actions.

He reconnoitered to the driftmouth closest to his target, first smearing himself with an extra covering of coal dust. His skin and clothes carried already so much filth that they could scarcely be darker, but he didn't want to leave anything to chance. He checked his pistol. Three shots left.

He hunched just inside the shaft. The rubble of the office lay only a few hundred feet distant. A patrol worked its way down the street, and Baxter counted out ten minutes before another patrol followed. In its wake, he moved.

The sudden shift of speed billowed the clothes from his emaciated frame. He'd mastered ghostly footsteps so as to travel with the least disturbance. He reached the office and hid himself behind the remainder of a wall, peeking over it only long enough to confirm the patrol's receding position.

He searched the broken desk and all its drawers. He lifted wooden wreckage from the filing cabinet, opened it, found nothing. He checked the larger cabinet beside where the window used to be. Nothing in those drawers either. His time ran short. He sunk behind the wall again and saw the top of a cardboard cylinder protruding from debris beyond the office foundation. Spattered mud and moisture camouflaged the tube. He abandoned the cover of the wall. Lunging for the tube, yanking it loose, a shot crashed toward him from the head of the street. Baxter threw himself into motion, firing blindly backward as he ran. A larger fusillade cracked in reply, but he'd chosen his position wisely and was soon in the earth again. His re-entry of the sleeping chamber awoke the men.

"Where'd you go?" Garris said.

"I got the blueprints."

"What for?"

"Maybe they can tell us something." Everyone gathered around to pore over the documents. Baxter pointed at a network of tunnels running under the plain and marked off with large Xs. "What are these?"

"Old shafts," Garris said. "Dug-out seams, maybe."

Another man pointed to the Xs. "*Csukott*," he said. "*Gáz*." He placed his hands palms-up on the dirt and then raised them as he wiggled his fingers, coughing for effect. "*Metán*." He scratched two lines in the dirt to represent tunnels. Across one he piled small stones.

Across the other, he laid splinters of wood. He pointed to each in turn, then circled the one with the splinters.

To Garris, Baxter said, "What do you think? It could end this whole thing, if we can get in and out quick enough."

Garris grunted.

Baxter took a deep breath. "I say we try it."

~

A long mainway ran north-south with the shuttered tunnels branching perpendicularly from it, extending under the plain. The blueprints indicated that the mainway was safe. Only the branch tunnels were not. Each man was allotted a certain number of tunnels, with Baxter's tally reduced because of his injury. Each man worked alone, his pack filled to bursting with large charges and long spools of wire. Baxter labored as effectively as possible with his wounded arm bound in a sling.

He never risked an open flame near the boarded-over shafts. He was wary even of his headlamp. At his final tunnel, he tied the end of the wire to his belt and set the sack of charges down immediately to his left. Mentally, he made note of the medium-sized rock beside the sack. He shut off his headlamp. Darkness enveloped him. He was blind.

He groped the face of the planks to determine where they met the walls. He smashed the rock into the center of the planking. The wood splintered. Baxter touched where the rock had impacted. He was not able to reach through. He smashed the planks again. This time the rock fell clear to the other side. A draft from the long-closed tunnel lapped at him. He tore back on the planks, ripping himself a large enough opening.

He rechecked the wire for good measure, pushed the sack of charges through the hole and followed it. The closed tunnels ran straight beneath the plain, so he did not worry about losing his way, but he was concerned about breaking the wire and thereby wasting an entire string of charges. He clambered over a small rockfall and walked carefully, estimating the distance to beneath the guard's camp. When he arrived, he began laying charges.

The gas thickened as he moved deeper into the tunnel. He began to feel dizzy. He kept working. Soon, he was coughing, but his charges were marching away, properly strung together. He didn't want to retreat before he finished. As he wrapped wire around contact points, he thought of what lay above his head, or what he hoped lay above his head. They'd not been able to measure precisely the quantity of rock between the camp on the surface and the charges below. Topside might do no more than shiver.

With the last charge in his hand, violent coughs took possession of him. His body racked like a tenement in a strong gust. He felt along the wall and found a crevice from which he cleared away dust and loose debris with his fingers. There, he set his final bomb. Turning away, he moved back toward the entrance as hurriedly as possible, his head a swamp of methane. The rockfall under his hands brought relief. He grasped again the splintered boards, and they felt like the gates to a holy city. He sat down in the mainway to rest.

~

He reached the central room before Garris, though a few other men had returned from sapping. Baxter began to change the dressing on his arm, unwrapping the wound for another cleaning when Garris at last arrived.

Garris said, "Any better?"

"It's been sore the last few days, but it hurts a lot less now. It just feels heavy. That's not good, is it?"

"Show."

The once red flesh had turned brown and in some places black. "And listen to this," Baxter said. The browned skin emitted a faint crackling when he pressed on it.

Garris looked away, swallowing hard with disgust. "It's turned on you. It's gonna kill you if you don't get rid of it." He whistled, and the other men came toward him. Baxter held out his gangrenous arm. Santino remained among the living. He winced when he saw the wound. "*Durante il servizio militare ho imparato up po' di medicina.*"

"I heard *medicina*," Baxter said.

"You want him or me to cut it off?" Garris asked.

"Him, I guess. Santino." Baxter made a chopping motion over the wound. "Can you do it?"

Santino drew a long, grave breath. He ran a hand through his hair, but then nodded.

Baxter looked down at the wound again. "I just don't want to be awake for it."

"There's whiskey left from when we hit the saloon."

Baxter drank until he lost consciousness. He awoke in the stope with only Garris and Santino present, the room lit by the butterfly wings of the lantern flame. He was lying down, his head pulsing just out of phase with his heartbeat.

"It's gone," Garris said.

Still half drunk, Baxter carefully lifted his right arm, which now ended at his elbow. Blood darkened the bandage. The arm felt horribly light. He tried to sit up, but a wave of dizziness and nausea flattened him.

"It came off quick, in only a couple of minutes," Garris said. "You almost woke up in the middle. Started groaning, but then you went back under. From the pain, I guess."

"I don't remember."

"Better that way. Santino tried to sew you up right. By and by he got you tied off, but you bled like a shoat. We thought you'd never stop."

~

At dawn and so dizzy that he had to hold to Garris for support, Baxter made his way to a high driftmouth where the others had already gathered. Wires were attached to batteries in an orderly assembly. Below, Lind's encampment huddled lonely and small on the plain. Plumes of smoke betrayed the fires which at night fluttered tenuously orange.

"Set to go," Garris said.

Baxter craned his head from the driftmouth. Dawn painted the sky. He saw the corral of horses set off from the tents, tried to calculate whether any of the charges lay beneath it. He could not properly estimate from so far away. Helpful, he thought, if a few horses survive. "Should we wait longer?" Baxter said.

"Whoever's in camp now ain't likely to stay much longer. Soon they'll be out patrolling."

Baxter said, "I guess it's time."

Garris touched two wires together.

The valley leaped.

The north side of the camp inflated with brown-tinged fire. The ground arched and threw soil and heat to the air. A squall of mud and rocks fell as Garris joined another two wires and a great fist crashed through the south end of the camp, sending tents skyward and into flame. The driftmouth grew raucous with cheering, but Garris didn't participate. He focused on the wires with a calm, intense absorption. Another two wires turned the near side of the camp to a pot of earth instantly aboil, throwing off tents, men, sections of town buildings abutting the camp, and leaving intact only the camp's eastern flank. A clutch of guards fled to the corral and pulled horses from a circling panic as the tethered ones, wretched and terrorized, ripped at their bonds, desperate for release.

"Last one up," Garris said.

Baxter said, "There are men in the corral."

"Too bad for them." Garris triggered the string of charges, and another mushroom of ground swelled and burst, tattering the final structures in the camp. The air released its debris, and the only visible movements were mounted men, already distant, tearing away to the east along the tracks so long empty now of trains.

Resting, his breathing steady and labored with relief or resignation, Garris said, "That's the works," and Baxter noticed how with shocking speed the mud-rain, the explosions, the men in the driftmouth, all subsided. The calm stunned him. Garris said, "In a while we'll head out, scout around."

Baxter agreed. He grimaced from a bolt of pain that shot up his arm and ricocheted through his entire body. He thought for a moment that he would pass out, but he held on, outlasting the worst, feeling a bit more of his life drain away. He'd not slept the previous night after emerging from his whiskey stupor. Garris had offered to stay awake with him for company. Baxter refused. He would simply have to sweat through his pain.

His stump became a thumping engine. He was so lightheaded that he feared he might lose his senses permanently. Two hundred miles to Denver, maybe fewer to the first working telegraph. The fleeing men would ride their horses to death and wire news to New York. Then the old man would arrange the next round. Lind and winter hadn't solved the problem. Now more drastic measures would be warranted. Powerful men would be notified and set on alert, urged into action.

"Stay here while we scrounge," Garris said.

"Not on your life," Baxter said.

He joined the grim reclamation. The wind drew aside curtains of smoke to reveal breathtaking destruction. The gas had blown with incredible force. Carriage-sized boulders had mixed with the dirt. Bodies, pieces of them, sprawled about. A dead man, upright but missing his body below the waist, perched on a rock where an explosion had deposited him. His arms hung calmly down, and his rictus defeated every one of Baxter's attempts to give it more than a glance. On the ground, a hand here, a head there. Very soon Baxter thought, these once-men will swell under the sun and begin to strain themselves with gasses and fluids. Their faces will sink into their skulls. Their lips will bloat and melt. The camp of charred soil and stones smelled of death and a rotten, sweet wetness. Baxter fought nausea.

The corral had not capped directly any of the charges and had survived mostly intact. The gate swung freely on its hinges. The horses bound to the fencing had calmed themselves since the blasts. Lucky. Healthy horses, an incalculable benefit.

The men rummaged for the better part of the morning, collecting burned blankets, canteens, a few ration packets. Everyone took care not to stumble into the cavernous holes left by the explosions. The cloths they tied around their mouths could not stanch the smell of earth and scattered meat. Periodically, a man paused to vomit, and eventually Baxter was called by Garris to a far corner of the field. He picked his way, eyes to the ground to keep his footing and not overlook any items of value. At Garris' location, he froze. Lind lay on the ground, legs pinned beneath a large stone tossed up by one of the bombs. His scorched clothes showed his skin in places, and dirt blackened his face. Unconscious. Clearly alive. His chest hitched in short, irregular gasps.

Baxter knelt. Lind's exposed skin was blistered, and both of his legs were kinked at grotesque angles.

"I'll hang around if you want me to," Garris said, "but I ain't helpin'. This one's on you."

"I'd like some water," Baxter said.

"I'll fetch you some." Garris turned his back and walked away.

For a long time Baxter simply stared. Then he salvaged Lind's coat and boots, gun, shells, gloves, his stinking socks. He stuffed everything into a burlap sack. His legs trembled. He began to cry. He could not help himself. He had come too easily to the decision about what to do next, and he felt no weakening of resolve. He chose a large rock nearby, a rock too big for him to handle with one arm. Clumsily, he used his stump for assistance. The rock dug through his bandage, touching off a blaring, sustained note of pain. He did not care. As his stump hemorrhaged, blood spread across one side of the rock and dripped into the dirt. He held the rock high and brought it down once. Then he brought it down again and again until he could not lift it anymore.

He couldn't taste saliva, only tears that he licked as they fell. He felt something apart from pleasure. The sensation of the dropping rock, of its contact with its target, warmed him, suffused him with momentary light, opened him to life. His heart was wrapped with mink because he had taken this life. He fell back on his heels. He watched the plain in silence as, on the horizon, a black wall rose and rushed toward him with precipitous haste.

A switching station near the east anchorage of the bridge. A small ticket counter.

"I can get you the tickets to Denver. Any farther, you have to ask locally. Also, you gotta go to Grand Central to board." The cashier stooped and came up with two brochures. "Pick your style."

The Expedition Flyer and the Twentieth Century Limited. The first, a ninety-mile-per-hour Chicago run with many stops along the way, an initial leg stretching to two days. The Century: faster, more luxurious. New York to Chicago in twenty hours. The brochure promised plush seating, separate dining and sleeping cars, secretarial services, a telegraph, even a barbershop. Expensive. He chose the Century. Time mattered. No one at the company would question the decision.

"Three, please. Two adults and a child."

Had I chosen the other train, he thought, *what of fate? A slower trip, chances for delays, a warped track, an emergency stop for an old man's heart condition. Something. A pause long enough for the strike to commence before my arrival.*

Packed and not yet tired, they arrived forty-five minutes early. Park Avenue and East 42nd. Eager to be on their way. Baxter checked their baggage one last time. He admired the arched windows framed in granite and limestone. Just opened in February with a midnight ceremony. Invited guests and the city fathers watched the old man cut the ribbon. The mayor was upstaged by the building's funder, who would not be denied. *The Metropolitan called it a monumental gateway, the glory of the city. Baxter could not wait to show it to Lorraine and Thomas. He tapped his son on the shoulder and pointed up at the sculpture of Mercury fifty feet high and sixty wide. Thomas craned his neck and gawked.*

Inside, a sudden shift in light. The main concourse resolved itself gradually. Ninety-foot-high double-glazed walls framed both ends. Glass-floored walkways. Electrification eliminated the soot, steam, and racket of the old stations. The terminal thronged with passengers, baggage handlers, cab drivers. Passages to the subways funneled people from incoming tracks. Near the outgoing, long-distance tracks, ticket agents, baggage checkers, and stores plied for last minute spending.

"It's wonderful!" Lorraine exclaimed.

"Isn't it? Isn't it?" Baxter said. "The old man is a genius. It's going to revolutionize the whole East Side."

They boarded their train, and Baxter found a seat in the leisure car where Thomas could sit on his lap and look out the window. Trains entered the station on the west side and looped to the eastern or midpoint platforms for departures. Great hotels rose around the terminal. The Roosevelt. The Manhattan. The Belmont. The Vanderbilt. The whole city regenerating, pressing forward in stone.

24

He awoke on the stoop of the supply shop. He felt rough planks against his back and realized he was sitting up. Garris squatted before him as he floundered into consciousness. Baxter looked down at his stump. A new wad of cloth had been secured to it. The pain returned. He remembered what he'd done, the reason for the fresh dressing. His insides felt cinched and empty. Through a cough, he asked, "How long did I bleed this time?"

"You sprung a good leak. Santino had to singe you shut. But don't waste time thinking about it." Garris hooked his arms under Baxter's armpits, lifted him halfway to his feet. "Gotta scat."

"I'm dead weight now. Put me down."

Garris tried to set Baxter right on his feet. "We ain't leavin' you here."

"Think for a moment. It makes no sense to take me along."

"Don't matter. It's worth the risk."

"I can be more help here if the troops come. They'll thrash me a little, which will slow them down."

Garris' mouth pulled into a frown. He acceded, and Baxter felt himself being lowered, released.

Garris walked from the porch to the remaining men and horses in the street. The horses' backs supported crude, stuffed saddlebags fashioned from burlap. Garris assembled a ration. Two canteens of water, blankets, lentils. "Space it out right. Should hold you for a few days." He offered a pistol.

Baxter said, "Take the bullets out. All but one."

"You take them out on your own if you want to. My advice is to keep that gun full and use it the way it's supposed to be used."

"I'll do what I can," Baxter said, "but the faster you go, the less chance they'll have of finding you."

Garris held one arm in the other, scratching at his elbow. His eyes swept across the ground. "Hell of a way to end up."

"Try to stay out of sight," Baxter said.

"Nothin' more invisible than niggers and poor men." Garris walked to his horse and climbed up unsteadily. The group headed south, teetering on the alien ground of the saddles. Baxter watched for as long as possible before all turned west and disappeared over the ridge.

He lost firm track of the number of days he spent on the porch. Dizziness, nausea, and sleep arrived of their own accord and on their own private schedules. He stilled himself in a vain attempt to hide from delirium. His arm unified with aches at one moment. At others, he wanted to tear off the bandage and plunge his fingers into the healing, itching flesh. Through times of lucidity, he saw himself from a distance, a lone figure motionless amidst smoldering ruins, a hermit or ghost too depleted to move.

Ravens and vultures colonized the valley. The vultures circled down in long, unhurried corkscrews. The plain was ripe with death and rot. Soon, the long season of dry heat would come and then winter again. Time and black birds would perform their sanitations.

When he felt strong enough to eat, he took small bites of lentils. He drank the water carefully and sat close enough to the edge of the stoop to have to move only minimally to accommodate his innards. The spring sun warmed him through the days. He could not escape the cloud of his own stench, but exposure accustomed him to it. One blanket sufficed against the daytime wind and sun. A second blanket sufficed for the nights. He fell asleep to crickets and the occasional swoop of an owl hunting rodents amid the rubble. He thought of Garris and the rest moving deeper into the canyons, perhaps soon clear through to Nevada or south to New Mexico.

At dawn, an unspecifiable dawn, he awoke to the sound of horses and men on the march. He assured himself he was not hallucinating. He saw soldiers clad in matching gray uniforms with brass buttons and wide belts. Not company guards. Not Pinkertons. Bayonets flashed from the rifles slung across their backs. The soldiers spread through the valley, guns and sabers drawn, panning their heads, searching. Baxter took up the pistol. He'd fired it twice to scare away coyotes. Now he considered using it again. He found that he didn't want to. He threw it from the stoop. Some time passed before a knot of soldiers spied him and galloped forward.

One man dismounted, his horse still trotting. A blonde, mustached man who didn't reach for his pistol. Uniform, clean. Medals, bright. He looked in his mid-forties and approached without fear. Baxter tried to speak. He only coughed.

"Easy," the blonde man said. He took Baxter's hand in his own. "Dearborn. I'm guessing you're Baxter?"

Baxter cleared his throat. "Yes," he croaked.

"Any of your friends still around, Mr. Baxter?"

"They're all dead."

Dearborn looked him up and down. "How long have you been sitting here?"

"A while. Days."

"We would have come sooner," Dearborn said, "but the bridge was all blown to hell halfway out of Denver. We had to mount up and ride from there."

A wisp of satisfaction passed over Baxter's face.

"What about your friends, Baxter? Are they still around?"

"They're all dead. I told you."

"So you have," Dearborn said. "But you can understand why that's a little hard for me to believe. It's only fair to tell you that if you say you're alone and we find out you're not, I'm going to have to make your life more difficult. Care to tell us what we'll find in those tunnels?"

"Coal. Maybe some bodies, though we dragged out as many as we could. What do you think those birds are feeding on?"

Dearborn turned toward the blasted camp where vultures humped about like lame, pot-bellied undertakers. "Filthy creatures," Dearborn said. He stood again. To one of his assistants, he said, "I assume there's a jail somewhere."

"Yes, sir. Not much left of it though. Three busted walls and half a roof."

"What about the cell?"

"Still looks secure."

"I'm afraid we're going to have to lock you up, Baxter. Will that be all right?"

Baxter said nothing.

"Good." Dearborn signaled for two men. "Be careful with Mr. Baxter. He's injured."

~

That evening Baxter was dozing on a bare cot when Dearborn arrived with a tray of food. The aroma made Baxter's mouth explode with saliva. A roll and two large portions of ground meat steamed on the tray. Baxter swallowed hard.

"I tried not to wake you," Dearborn said.

"It didn't work."

"Don't be discourteous. There's no need. Stay where you are for the moment." Dearborn opened the cell and slid the tray just inside the door. Baxter moved forward, but Dearborn held up a hand. Baxter froze while Dearborn relocked the door. "All right," Dearborn said.

Baxter could not control himself. He shoveled the food in, too hungry to care what he looked like, each mouthful opening another chamber of his stomach. Every so often he glanced up, hoping to read his jailer in some way, but Dearborn had withdrawn to the edge of the blasted wall to look out onto the plain.

Suddenly, Baxter stopped. He spat out what remained in his mouth and pushed the tray away in a clanging skid.

"It's all right," Dearborn said without turning. "It's not poisoned or drugged. Don't worry."

Baxter did not move. Dearborn faced him. "Go ahead," he said. "Toss me that roll. I'll eat it if you don't believe me. I don't start out with lies or torture. I give a man the opportunity to tell me the truth. Then I verify. What verification tells me determines my subsequent course of action."

Baxter approached the food again, scraped at it, and soon finished. "Thank you," he said.

"Nobody's ever starved on my watch."

Baxter closed his eyes. His body slumped in near ecstasy from the food even as his stomach pinched with cramps. He burped and excused himself.

"Quite all right," Dearborn said. His eyes were weary, sad, cradled with flesh. "We've been looking around."

"What did you find?"

"So far, bodies, black, white. More or less what you said."

"And what's going to happen now?"

"Nothing for a few days. We have to finish the search, assess the damage, get the telegraph up and running again if we can. Routine, in other words. Is there anything you'd like?"

"Just leave me alone, please."

"Of course," Dearborn said. "If you need anything, be sure to ask. I can't promise it will be delivered, but your request will be heard. There's a guard outside, naturally."

"Dearborn."

"Yes?"

"You would have done exactly as I did."

"Probably, but that makes no difference."

~

He was left mostly to solitude. Dearborn intruded with brief, twice-daily deliveries of food. Baxter was provided with a large bucket in which to relieve himself. The clean-faced recruit to whom Dearborn delegated the duty of removing Baxter's waste was understandably gloomy and resentful. Once, he spat on Baxter after taking up the bucket. Baxter did not report him. He bore the young man no grudge. Baxter grew cold, and Dearborn helped him. They talked of the past until the subject forced them to silence. Such talking, such uncontrollable pryings at his mind. Dearborn knew something. Baxter swept away words and felt more comfortable.

The wait coiled around him. Night issued a mouse which scurried through the bars, cheeked a crumb of something edible and paused to sniff at him twice before turning back and going on its way. The mouse loosed his despair. He began to sob, unable to control his volume. Dearborn did not interrupt him.

Dawn. Then, in the evening, a shower passed over the valley. The rain trickled before falling for minutes like a slide of gravel. In the canyons the storm might spawn freshets from which Garris and the others could drink. Baxter smelled wet air mixed with earth, knew the dry places of the world could be touched by fecundity. The pleasure was short-lived. Another night like the previous two. No ceremony, just recollections upon recollections, his heart tearing at itself, stalemating and beginning again. He wondered in the morning whether Dearborn would come for him. He knew he would not be able to stand for very long. He wanted to walk unassisted from the cell. He sat on the cot and waited. Sunrise came and went. The stirrings of another day's reprieve. Then, boots on the wooden floor and Dearborn before the bars with a short length of rope.

"Well?" Baxter asked.

"We've searched to my satisfaction. You told the truth. I thank you for that."

So it's *this* morning, Baxter thought.

"I have something for you," Dearborn continued. "We got the wire up and running again. I informed my superiors that you were found alive. A few hours later a message came back for you."

Baxter read the telegram.

> YOU HAVE MADE YOUR DESERT BAXTER STOP NOW I WILL
> HAVE MY PEACE STOP
>
> P.D.R.

He offered the message to Dearborn.

"None of my business. I don't read other people's mail. Fold it up again and hand it to me." Baxter did as he was told. Dearborn struck a match and burned the paper.

"I'd like to send a reply," Baxter said.

"Of course." Dearborn passed him a scrap of paper and a pencil. Left-handed now, Baxter scrawled:

> RUAT CAELUM

He folded the paper in half and gave it to Dearborn. "For Mr. Robertson, please."

"I'll do my best," Dearborn said. He held up the rope. "We're going to move you to another building. Time to secure you for that."

Baxter came to the bars.

"Turn around, please," Dearborn said. Reaching into the cell, he bound Baxter's uninjured arm. "Step away from the door, please." Baxter complied, and Dearborn opened the cell. "All right," Dearborn said. Baxter walked out into the mud behind the building.

"Stop," Dearborn said.

Baxter stopped. He felt no anxiety. The rope dug into his side. Otherwise, he registered no remarkable sensations. His thoughts silted over. He reached into the muck and pulled out the azure bowl of Grand Central's ceiling, its twenty-five hundred painted stars, the constellations glinting with electric lights, and his wife and son, beaming.

Dearborn's pistol clicked as he prepared it for use.

"I won't kneel," Baxter said.